"It's almost dark. I'd like to go back to the castle now," Ysabel said softly.

"I thought I could work with you here. I thought I could shut you out—but it's not working anymore."

"I haven't done anything to disturb you."

"Which disturbs me more than anything you could do. You sit there with your hands folded and your expression serene as a madonna's, and I want to break something." He got up and moved slowly toward her. "I want to hear you yell at me. I want to see you without that blasted armor."

He was now so close she could see the pupils of his glittering eyes and feel the heat of his body reaching out and enfolding her. She couldn't breathe. "I don't know what you mean. I have no armor."

"You do." He reached out and trailed his index finger down her throat, leaving a path of fire in its wake. "But any armor can be pierced with the right weapon." His thumb settled in the hollow of her throat, testing the tempo of her heart. "You like my touching you?"

Like was not the word, she thought in bewilderment. His touch produced a pleasure so intense, it was close to pain.

"Let's see what else you like." His head slowly lowered as his hand moved down to caress her body. "Open your mouth."

Her body was responding, heating, clenching under the onslaught of his hands.

"Open," he repeated softly.

She closed her eyes and obeyed him. As his mouth claimed hers, his fingers unzipped the back of her dress and lowered it to her waist. "Give me more, Ysabel. . . ."

WHAT ARE *LOVESWEPT* ROMANCES?

They are stories of true romance and touching emotion. We believe those two very important ingredients are constants in our highly sensual and very believable stories in the *LOVESWEPT* line. Our goal is to give you, the reader, stories of consistently high quality that may sometimes make you laugh, sometimes make you cry, but are always fresh and creative and contain many delightful surprises within their pages.

Most romance fans read an enormous number of books. Those they truly love, they keep. Others may be traded with friends and soon forgotten. We hope that each *LOVESWEPT* romance will be a treasure—a "keeper." We will always try to publish

LOVE STORIES YOU'LL NEVER FORGET
BY AUTHORS YOU'LL ALWAYS REMEMBER

The Editors

Loveswept ® 522

Iris Johansen
Winter Bride

BANTAM BOOKS
NEW YORK · TORONTO · LONDON · SYDNEY · AUCKLAND

WINTER BRIDE

A Bantam Book / February 1992

ISBN 0-553-44186-8

Published simultaneously in the United States and Canada

PRINTED IN THE UNITED STATES OF AMERICA

OPM   0 9 8 7 6 5 4 3 2 1

Winter Bride

One

Jed Corbin possessed a face that riveted attention and a deep voice he played like a musical instrument, projecting notes of humor, sternness, and crisp decisiveness with faultless symmetry. He bore no resemblance to Arnold at all, Ysabel realized with profound relief.

"It's time you went to bed now." The command came from outside the library where Ysabel sat. "I've made you a cup of hot chocolate and set it on your nightstand in your room. What are you—" Betty Starnes stopped in the doorway, her gaze fastened with shock on the face of the man on the big-screen TV. "Jed," she muttered.

Ysabel's finger went instinctively to the off switch of the remote control before she realized it was no longer necessary to hide her interest in Jed Corbin. "You were here before he left, weren't you? Did he look like this when you knew him?" Ysabel leaned forward, absorbed with catching the expressions flickering across the journalist's mobile face.

"No, he was only twenty-two and his hair was black, not silver . . . and his expression is harder now." Betty tore her gaze from the television to stare accusingly at Ysabel. "You shouldn't be ogling that imp of Satan. You know Mr. Arnold wouldn't like it."

"He's broadcasting from Paris tonight. He seems quite competent." She added casually, "I just ran across the program." Was she afraid to tell Betty the truth? she wondered. It was none of the housekeeper's business that Ysabel had purposely arranged to watch Jed Corbin tonight, but the habits ingrained over the years were hard to break.

She tried to block the waves of disapproval the woman was projecting as she hit the mute button on the remote control. That was better. Jed Corbin's deep mesmerizing voice was having a disturbing effect and interfering with her concentration. A perfectly natural reaction, she thought quickly. She had never been permitted to watch him on television, but from what she had read in the papers he had the same effect on millions of other viewers.

Jed Corbin was the foremost news anchorman in the United States and though he had built his reputation on a combination of sound journalism and breathtaking fearlessness, his magnetic physical appeal must have been a valuable asset to him. Twenty-two, Betty had said. That meant he was only thirty-six now, and his close-cropped silver hair was definitely premature. It was difficult to imagine him with dark hair or with any hint of softness clinging to him. His tan face was lined by experience, and his light blue eyes gazed out at her with weary cynicism. Dressed in a cream-colored cable-knit sweater and tweed sport coat, he was as different from the elegant, thoughtful anchorman Ysabel regularly watched as a tiger was from a pussy cat.

"Competent? The only thing Jed Corbin's competent at is causing trouble." Betty marched over to the television, her tall, powerful body quivering with indignation. She turned off the set. "I can't believe you did this. You were told that man's program was never to be watched in this house. Here, poor Mr. Arnold has been in his grave only two days and already you're flaunting his orders."

"Betty, I'd like to see—" Ysabel broke off as she saw the woman's determined expression. The housekeeper would have to learn the status quo had changed, but Ysabel was too weary to fight her at the moment. The last six months of Arnold's life had drained her strength and stamina, and she must save herself for the important battles. "Very well." She obediently rose to her feet and started toward the door. "By the way, I phoned Lyle Townsend late this afternoon, but his secretary said he'd have to return my call. Make sure he's put through to me even if I'm already asleep."

"Why would you call him?"

The question was spoken with Betty's usual blunt curiosity, but Ysabel ignored her rudeness. "He's Arnold's lawyer. I thought I'd ask him to come to the castle tomorrow to have a discussion concerning the will."

"You know what's in the will. He read it to you in this very room right after the funeral."

Ysabel carefully restrained the flicker of annoyance she felt. She had learned to control her anger, suppress her true nature, and it was not time to release either. "I'd still like to go over a few of the clauses with him." She wished Betty would just accept her words without questioning. Lies did not come easily to her. Heaven knows, her life in this house would have been a good deal easier if they had.

"You shouldn't trouble your head about such business. Mr. Townsend will take care of everything for you just as he did for Mr. Arnold."

Ysabel forced a smile. "But it's my duty to at least have a superficial idea of Arnold's holdings."

"Maybe," Betty acceded grudgingly. "Okay, I'll put through the call."

"Thank you." Ysabel kept the sarcasm from her tone. She moved toward the stone steps leading to the second floor of the castle. "Good night, Betty."

"You remember to drink your hot chocolate. You need it to help you sleep."

Ysabel knew Betty didn't care a whit about whether she slept well or not. The chocolate was just another way of enforcing her will on Ysabel. Arnold had taught his housekeeper well the ways of tyranny. "Yes, of course."

As she climbed the steps she noticed how softly and fluidly the skirt of her ivory-colored velvet robe flowed over the cold gray stone. How she had grown to hate these lounging robes Arnold had insisted she wear these past seven years. The gowns had become a symbol of her bondage as much as Betty's arrogant, bullying presence. But her imprisonment was nearly over. Soon she would be able to fully concentrate on the purpose that had obsessed her all these years, and both the symbols and chains would go up in smoke.

And Jed Corbin could well be the flame that would burn through the links.

"Now, mind you go right to bed," Betty called after her.

Ysabel smiled serenely but didn't look at her as she lifted her skirts with the quaint, graceful gesture Arnold had taught her, and proceeded up the stairs. "Don't I always do what you tell me?"

"A Mr. Townsend to see you, Monsieur Corbin," the concierge announced as soon as Jed picked up the phone. "Shall I send him up?"

"No problem. Townsend called me from the airport. I'm expecting him." Jed hung up and immediately the phone rang again.

Ronnie's voice practically burst over the line. "Jed, I just saw you on television. What the hell do you think you're doing? You told me you were going on vacation too."

"Calm down, Ronnie. That's why I'm doing the series in Paris. It's almost a vacation."

"The devil it is. You send me to Puerto Rico and then go off on a job. I'm sick to death of all this sunshine and sand and—"

"Only you would complain about lying on a tropical beach for two months."

"Beaches are boring."

"Everything is boring to you but your camera.

You needed this vacation. The doctor said you hadn't let yourself recuperate fully after you got out of the hospital in Kuwait."

"Bull. I'll be watching you. You do another broadcast and you'll find me knocking on your door." Ronnie hung up.

That's all he needed, Jed thought ruefully. He should have known Ronnie would start chomping at the bit the minute it became clear Jed hadn't taken a break as he had said he was going to do.

He replaced the receiver and went back to his packing.

A knock sounded on the door. Townsend.

Jed glanced through the peephole to be sure. He hadn't seen the man for over fourteen years but had no trouble recognizing him. The lawyer was a little more plump, his graying hair receding, but he could swear the dark blue Brooks Brothers suit was the same one he had worn when he had arranged bail for Jed after that barroom brawl in Tacoma.

He swung open the door. "Come in, Townsend. But you'll have to be brief." He strode across the room and closed the suitcase. "You've caught me at a bad time. I've ordered a taxi to pick me up in fifteen minutes."

"So that inquisitive young person downstairs informed me." Townsend seemed faintly disgruntled. "She did everything but take my fingerprints before allowing me to come up and see you."

"Good. I'm glad she followed through with my orders. I like my privacy." He fastened the snaps on the suitcase. "Talk fast, Townsend."

Townsend came into the room and closed the door. "I've flown all the way from Seattle to see you. I would think you could allow me a few moments of your precious time."

"I am allowing you a few moments." Jed grinned at him over his shoulder as he unplugged his laptop computer on the desk. "A very few moments. I'm sure anything my father has to communicate through you can be said in verbal shorthand."

"Your father is dead."

Jed halted in midmotion. He had known this news would come sometime, but he hadn't expected the shock and rush of undefinable emotions flooding through him. "When?"

"A week ago. He suffered a heart attack over two years ago and was bedridden until his demise last week. We would have contacted you earlier, but it was his wish we not advise you of his illness."

"I see." He snapped the lid of his laptop shut. "Is that all you wanted to tell me?"

"Not quite. It's my duty to inform you your father left none of his considerable fortune to you."

"I never expected he would. My father hated my guts from the time I was old enough to see him for what he was." Jed placed the laptop in its case and set it beside the suitcase on the bed. "Arnold Corbin had an aversion for truth in any form."

"You shouldn't speak ill of the dead."

"It's no more than I've said to his face." Jed shrugged on his tweed sport jacket. "Which is more honesty than you gave him."

"Our firm was always most conscientious regarding the management of your father's affairs."

"And you detested him."

"I didn't say . . ." Townsend met Jed's gaze and slowly nodded. "I didn't realize you knew of my dislike. Arnold Corbin was not a pleasant individual."

Jed experienced surprise and then a flicker of grudging respect. The man had more integrity than he remembered. Hell, the wild kid he'd been back then probably wouldn't have been able to make an unbiased judgment of any of his father's minions. He'd been too full of hurt and resentment and distrust. "He was a selfish bastard who didn't care who he hurt as long as he got what he wanted," Jed said bluntly. "You know it and I know it."

"Yes." A small smile touched Townsend's lips. "I must admit I was rather glad to hear you did so well after you broke with him and left the castle. Your success was a source of great rage and disappointment to him." He lifted his brows inquiringly. "I imagine you have no real need for his money?"

"No need at all. I could have bought and sold him anytime in the past five years." Jed smiled grimly. "And I would have taken great pleasure in doing it, but I didn't want anything that belonged to my father."

"How fortunate for you." Townsend hesitated. "Then I'm afraid my journey is going to prove futile. I was asked to put a request to you."

Jed turned to look at him. "Request?"

"Your stepmother sent me. She was the sole beneficiary but suggests you meet with her to discuss a possible settlement in return for a certain favor she intends to ask of you."

Jed laughed mirthlessly. "Good God, what next? Cherry and I were never close enough to exchange favors"—he smiled crookedly—"though she offered me a few interesting invitations before I left the castle. The only reason I didn't take advantage of them was that I knew she was too dumb to realize my father would kick her out on her derriere when he found out."

"Cherry?" Townsend frowned, puzzled.

"My voluptuous but slightly dim-witted stepmother," Jed said impatiently.

"Oh, no," the lawyer stated. "Your father divorced Cherry Winston Corbin some time ago. He'd married twice afterward. His widow and beneficiary is Ysabel Belfort Corbin."

"Stepmother number five," Jed murmured. "I should have realized. . . . His women never lasted more than a year or two. And what does the lady want from me?"

"I have no idea. She didn't give me her confidence. She only asked me to see you personally and request you come to her."

"Well, you've made your request. Tell her she has nothing to offer me that I need."

"I thought as much." Townsend sighed. "But I had to try. I felt a little sorry for the young woman."

"Why?" Jed smiled. "She's obviously going to be a very rich widow. How long did she stick with the bastard?"

"Seven years."

Jed gave a low whistle. "Then she deserves every penny."

"More than you know. Toward the end of your father's illness her life was almost unbearable."

"But she had such a bright golden future to look forward to, didn't she?"

"I don't believe . . ." Townsend hesitated. "I don't think she married him for his money."

Jed laughed incredulously. "You're saying she cared about him?"

"I didn't say that. She just doesn't impress me as the kind of woman who . . . She's not like the others."

"And what is she like?"

"A quiet little thing, rather fragile, almost other-worldly." Townsend's lips tightened. "Your father bullied her unmercifully. She was little more than a slave to him."

"A very pampered slave, I'm sure. Beautiful?"

"Exceptionally."

"Then she had a ticket to leave at any time. Beautiful women are welcomed wherever they go. She chose to stay with the bastard." He gathered up his cases and headed for the door. "My taxi is waiting."

"Then your answer is an unequivocal no?"

"I thought I'd made that clear," Jed said as he opened the door. "Even if I were tempted to go back to the castle, I have more on my plate right now than I can handle."

Townsend followed him. "She appears rather desperate. I'm sure she would comply to almost any terms you'd care to offer. Winter Castle is quite a valuable property."

"Who would buy it? It was only a monument to my father's vanity and king complex. No one wants turrets and drawbridges in this day and age. It's as much an anachronism as the London Bridge they stuck out in that Arizona desert."

"What about Winter Island itself? An island within a twenty-minute boat ride to Seattle is a very valuable . . ." He trailed off as he saw Jed shake his head. "You're sure there's nothing you'd like to have?"

"You're damn right I'm sure. What could she—" He stopped.

A woman wrapped in a white ermine-trimmed velvet cloak, her dark hair shimmering as brightly as the icicles hanging from the branches of the tree under which she was standing.

"You've thought of something?" Townsend asked.

Great dark eyes wide with apprehension as she looked at the castle on the hill.

He had willed himself to forget her but now he knew he never had.

And, great heavens, what a joke on his dear departed father. Arnold Corbin would be roaring in rage from hell at the idea of Jed owning his most valued possession. The image brought him a savage sense of satisfaction that astonished him. He had thought he had rid himself of the resentment and thirst for vengeance that had possessed him when he left the castle. Now they were back in full force, and it made no difference at all that his enemy had already been vanquished by the final antagonist. Why not? By God, he *would* have it!

"Yes, I've thought of something I want," Jed said softly. "Tell my dear stepmaman I can't come at once but to expect me." He closed the door and strode down the hall toward the elevators with Townsend at his heels. "She can definitely expect me."

Two

A hand clapped over Ysabel's mouth, jarring her from sleep.

"It's all right. Keep quiet. I have no intention of hurting you."

Darkness. Fear. Danger. *Guardia!*

Her eyes flew open, and her heart beat wildly. The palm sealing her lips was callused and hard. She was too terrified to register there was no brutality in the grasp.

She started to struggle, trying frantically to escape that smothering hand.

"I tell you it's okay. Just let me—"

Her teeth sank deep into his palm.

He gasped in pain and jerked his hand away. "Dammit, I told you I wasn't—"

She punched him in the midsection with her fist.

She heard a grunt of pain as she rolled out of bed

and onto the floor. She sprang to her feet and ran for the door leading to the hall.

He tackled her before she was halfway across the room, flipped her over on the floor, and straddled her.

"Listen to me. Just let me explain."

Something was vaguely familiar about his deep voice, but she had no time to analyze. Imprisoned between his thighs, she couldn't knee him, but her hands were still free and his genitals must be in reach. . . . Her fist struck hard, fast and accurate.

He groaned and collapsed on top of her, fumbling in the darkness for her wrists. He captured both of them and pinned her to the floor.

"Let me go or I swear I'll castrate you," she hissed.

"You damn near already did. I'll be more careful about accepting your next invitation to visit." The words were spoken in almost a growl, but the voice was as musical as the bass notes of a piano.

She *had* heard that voice before. She stopped struggling. "Who are you?"

"Your loving stepson." He raised himself to a sitting position astride her. "Jed Corbin. Will you attack me again if I turn your arms loose?"

"Of course not." Relief turned her every muscle weak. "Though it was entirely your own fault if I hurt you. When you frightened me, I acted instinctively."

"Then your instincts are fairly lethal," he said dryly. "And Townsend must be a lousy judge of character."

She was suddenly acutely conscious of the hardness of his thighs cradling her hips, the scent of soap and after-shave lotion drifting to her in the darkness. "Will you . . ." Her voice was slightly breathless and she paused to steady it. ". . . please get off me?"

"Since you ask so nicely." He didn't move and she became aware of a subtle change in his body, a sensual intonation in his voice. "Though I'm tempted to explore the situation further. I've never realized how close to the primitive we are in moments of conflict. It's very . . . arousing."

She felt a flutter of fear and stiffened, ready to attack again.

"For Lord's sake, I've no intention of raping you." A moment later his weight was gone and he was moving across the room toward the nightstand. "I just thought you might be similarly inclined."

"Why are you here?"

"You asked me to come."

"Not like this. Not in the middle of the night, with no warning or—"

"I just flew in from Paris and preferred our visit be private. Not that I imagined anyone would kill the fatted calf for me. I've never been made to feel particularly welcome here." He turned on the lamp on the nighstand and was immediately surrounded by a pool of soft light. "However, I didn't anticipate this kind of reception. I assumed Townsend's delicate little flower would give me a chance to explain before she swooned in terror."

He looked the same as he had on television and yet there were significant differences. He wasn't as tall as she had thought, barely six feet in height, but every inch was solidly knit. The faded jeans he wore outlined the heavy muscles of his thighs and the tight compactness of his buttocks, and the pushed-up sleeves of his black turtleneck sweat-shirt revealed tanned, powerful forearms. He appeared tougher. The aura he exuded was rougher, more reckless, and his face was more vibrantly alive beneath that cropped cap of silver hair.

"I'm sorry to have disappointed you." She sat up and got to her knees. "But I'm glad you came, Mr. Corbin."

He peered into the shadows where she knelt. "No complaints, no outrage at my rough treatment?"

"I'm sure you fared worse than I did."

"I'm sure too."

"How did you get here?"

"I rented a speed boat in Seattle and docked on the other side of the island." He squinted his eyes. "I can barely see you over there. What the hell are you wearing? Some kind of costume?"

"Just a robe." She stood up and tried to tidy her tousled hair. "I'd like to thank you for coming to hear me out. Suppose we get down to—"

He stiffened. "That's not just any robe." He suddenly muttered a curse, his ice-blue eyes glittering. "Come over here into the light where I can see you."

She hesitated and then moved slowly across the room toward him.

He watched her, his eyes narrowed, his stance strangely tense. "Well, I'll be damned," he murmured.

She stopped before him, bracing herself as his gaze traveled over the sleek lines of the long white velvet gown with its golden girdle to the matching gold braid on the flowering sleeves.

"The Winter Bride." He threw back his head and laughed uproariously but entirely without mirth. "Good God, I can't believe it." He grabbed her wrist and dragged her toward the door. "I've got to see you together. Is she still in the library?"

"Yes, but I don't want—"

He ignored her protest, pulling her down the hall and down the curved flight of steps.

"Please, there's no sense to this," she said quietly. "You've already seen . . . You know we're alike."

"I have to be sure." His harsh tone belied the smile baring his teeth. "Trust the old man to manage to get it all." He threw open the door to the library and switched on the overhead light, his gaze going to the painting over the fireplace. "He always did have the luck of the devil." He pulled her over to stand in front of the mantel. "Let's see just how lucky the bastard was."

She didn't have to glance at the painting to know what he was seeing. She knew every brush stroke, every shading of color. The anonymous artist had portrayed a young woman, scarcely more than a child, dressed in an ivory-colored medieval-style gown and ermine-trimmed cloak and standing alone beneath an ice-flocked tree. She was staring at the castle in the background, her eyes wide with fear and anticipation. Ysabel ignored the painting and stared at Jed Corbin. Dear God, he was angry, she realized in bewilderment. She could almost feel the furnace-hot waves of emotion he was exuding.

"Exquisite," he said softly, looking at her face. "Same marvelous bone structure, same impossibly long lashes, same dark eyes and hair." He reached out and touched her cheek with his forefinger. "Lord, even the textures are the same. Your skin feels just as silky as it looks in the picture."

Her skin seemed to burn beneath his touch, but it had to be her imagination.

His gaze moved down her throat to her breasts. "A little more voluptuous than the Bride's but that's not necessarily a bad thing, is it?" Something glinted, then burned in those light blue eyes. Another wave of anger seemed to have been ignited in him.

"Will you let me go please? You're hurting my wrist."

"I certainly wouldn't want to cause you discomfort. All brides should be treated with gentleness and care." He released her wrist and stepped back. "As I'm sure my father taught you."

She absently rubbed her wrist. "Why are you so angry?"

"I'm not—the *hell* I'm not." He drew a deep ragged breath. "He's won again. I thought I saw a way to get some of my own back, but he's blocked me again."

"I don't understand."

"He not only had his precious painting, he had the real Winter Bride." His movements were charged with barely contained violence as he strode across the room and threw himself in a chair. "Where the hell did he find you?"

"San Miguel."

"The island off the coast of South America?"

"Yes."

"You're a citizen of San Miguel?"

"My mother was a citizen, my father was American." She made an impatient gesture. "This has no importance. Can't we talk about why I've asked you to come here?"

"It's important to me." He touched his fingertips together in a Confucius-like gesture that should have looked serene; it didn't. "I find everything about this bizarre relationship between you and my father completely fascinating." His gaze ran over her. "My Lord, you look like someone from *A Connecticut Yankee in King Arthur's Court.* Did it titillate him to see you like this?"

She didn't answer.

"I'm sure it did. Seven years . . . How old are you now?"

"I can't see how—twenty-three."

His gaze shifted to the painting. "Practically a child bride. You must have looked even more like her then."

"Yes, I did."

"How lucky for you."

"Yes."

"And how long did it take my father to persuade you to join him in wedded bliss after you met?"

She didn't answer.

"How long?"

"Three days."

He threw back his head and laughed. "You obviously weren't as shy and retiring as our Winter Bride."

"I really don't wish to talk about it." She squared her shoulders. "You're clearly as obsessed with the painting as your father was, but I don't have to deal with your idiosyncracies."

"Oh, but you do." His hands dropped to the arms of the chair. "Because you want something from me just as you wanted something from my father. Why else am I here?"

He was right, she thought wearily. She needed him, and she had learned no one gave something for nothing. She had been prepared to pay, but she had not thought about what price would be demanded. She drew a deep steady breath and tried to wrap her usual cloak of serenity over her inner turbulence. "You're quite right, of course, Mr. Corbin. I do want something from you."

"Jed," he corrected. "After all, we're family, aren't we? Whatever it is you want, I'd judge you want it very badly, indeed."

She nodded. "Yes."

"You shouldn't admit that to me. It weakens your bargaining position."

"You'd probably see through me anyway." She added simply, "I'm not clever about this sort of thing."

His expression changed in some undefinable way. "I'm not as gullible as Townsend. You're not going to convince me you're helpless and ineffective." He grimaced as he glanced down at his lower body. "I have painful evidence to the contrary."

"I'm not helpless. I can protect myself."

"Oh yes."

"But that doesn't mean I'm capable of manipulation. I believe in being as straightforward as possible. It makes life much simpler."

"And were you straightforward with my father?"

"Absolutely."

"Interesting."

"You don't believe me?"

"As a matter of fact, I do." He smiled faintly. "I don't want to believe you, but I've done too many in-depth interviews not to spot a lie when I see one."

"Why don't you want to believe me?" Then she answered the question herself. "You resent me." Her brow wrinkled as she tried to puzzle it out. "You and your father had no liking for each other so you can't resent the fact you think I married him for his money."

"I would have been delighted if you'd taken him for every stock in his portfolio and sent him reeling to skid row."

"I see."

"No, you don't. What was between me and my father was complicated. It took me years to understand it."

"But I had nothing to do with the argument between you. Why do you—"

"Don't look for reason. My reaction is purely emotional." As she continued to stare at him he said harshly, "Stop looking at me so mournfully with those big black eyes. It bothers me."

"I'm sorry, I'm just trying to understand."

His lips tightened. "It's very simple. You gave him what he wanted most—you gave him his dream." He stood up and moved toward the door. "You're right, I do resent you."

He was leaving, she realized in panic. "Where are you going?"

"I have to digest this." His gaze went to the

painting. "I wasn't expecting this particular development when I came back here."

"But we have to talk. I need—"

"Not now. It wouldn't be wise. I'm so charged, I feel as if I'm about to detonate."

"Then when?"

"I'll come back tomorrow night."

"Where are you going? Back to the mainland?"

"There's a cottage on the other side of the island where I used to live after my father and I found we couldn't stand the sight of each other." His lips twisted. "I rather thought he'd have burned it like an effigy, but I saw it when I docked. Is it occupied?"

"I don't think so. I asked Arnold about it once, but he wouldn't talk about it. You could stay here. I could have Betty make up a room."

He paused. "Is that old harridan still here?"

"Yes, Arnold left her a legacy and instructions that she stay on here after his death."

"When she used to stalk around the castle, she reminded me of the giant's wife in 'Jack and the Beanstalk.'" He smiled crookedly. "I'm almost tempted to stay just to see her look of outrage when she catches me in these hallowed halls." He opened the door. "But, as I said, I prefer no one knows I'm here."

"But you'll be back. You promise?"

"Oh, I'll be back. I have a full measure of the newsman's usual insatiable curiosity. I couldn't walk out without all my questions answered."

"But you are walking out," she pointed out. "Why don't you stay and let me tell you what—"

"Sorry." His lips tightened. "I'm afraid you won't find me as pliant to your demands as my father."

"Pliant?" She gazed at him in bewilderment. "I was the one who had to be compliant."

Again his anger blasted at her from across the room. "And I'm sure you did it very well."

The door closed behind him before she could reply.

Pliant. She closed her eyes as memories flooded back to her of that forced compliance. No, she wouldn't think of Arnold. The long ordeal was over, and now she could make a new life for herself.

Her lids flicked open and she moved purposefully toward the door. Jed Corbin's arrival had brought problems she hadn't expected, but she would just have to make adjustments and find a way to convince him to do what had to be done. She was good at making adjustments, she thought bitterly. She had certainly had enough practice in the art.

The cottage was still there, nestling on the cliff like a disreputable sea gull after the peacock splendor of the castle.

He didn't need to break in; the door was unlocked and swung open to reveal dirt, mildew, and cockroaches scurrying across the moonlit floor in front of him. He played the beam of his flashlight around the small room.

Fourteen years. If the cottage had ever had another occupant, it wasn't evident at first glance. Even his well-thumbed copy of *War and Peace* was still on the bookshelf he'd fashioned on the far wall. Not surprising. Arnold had always hated the primitive cabin and ignored it—and Jed—whenever possible. The place had never had electricity, but there used to be an oil lamp on a chest.

After he had lit the lamp, he surveyed the room. Though badly in need of cleaning, airing, and probably debugging, it was more habitable than many of the places in the war-torn hot spots he'd slept in since he had left the island.

But he knew he wouldn't be able to sleep tonight.

He had told Ysabel the truth when he had left the castle. Lord, *left* wasn't the word. He had almost run away from the library and still felt as if he were about to explode. Seeing her had triggered an emotional overload.

His response had been so violent and out of proportion, he'd had to grab time to analyze and gain control. So analyze, dammit, he told himself. He wasn't a wild kid ruled by his passions any longer.

Yet he felt like that boy, angry and cheated and jealous. The first two emotions he could understand, but the jealousy?

It was the painting, he assured himself. She was right; it appeared he still retained his attachment for the painting. He had thought he had smothered his obsession along with the more bitter memories of the castle. All right, he still wanted the painting, but he wasn't his father and had no intention of transferring that passion from the child in the painting to her living likeness.

He deliberately pulled up the memory of Ysabel

as she had stood before him in the study. Tiny, fragile, her gaze wondering and yet serene, an air of patience and resignation surrounding her.

Yet she had been neither patient nor resigned when they had been struggling in the darkness. He had been conscious of a strength and determination that had caught him off guard. Her face might be identical to that of the Winter Bride, but she was no frightened child.

And when he had held her struggling, panting in the darkness, he had felt himself harden.

Lust. A primitive reaction to conquest and submission as he had told her. How could it be anything more when at that point he hadn't even seen her face?

Yet the reaction hadn't disappeared. As he had watched her standing by the mantel he had been swept by the same passion he had experienced when she had lain helpless between his thighs in the bedroom.

Emotions were seldom black and white, anger could have spilled over and formed a—

No, he wouldn't lie to himself. What he had felt had been lust, pure and simple. If lust was ever either pure or simple, he thought cynically. Whatever he had felt, he had to get it under control before he saw her again.

He moved quickly across the cottage to the closet where he had previously kept a broom and cleaning supplies. He needed an outlet for the emotion storming through him. He would clean and scrub the cottage until it was habitable and he was exhausted enough to sleep.

And he would not think about either the Winter Bride or Ysabel.

Ysabel was forcing herself to sit quietly in the Queen Anne chair beside her bed when Jed walked in on her the following day at two o'clock in the morning. She tensed, her hands nervously grasping the arms of the chair. She had been mentally preparing herself all day for this interview, but his presence instantly blasted all her plans to the four winds.

He was again dressed casually in jeans and a dark green crew neck sweater that made his hair gleam like polished pewter. And he was clearly in no better humor than when he had left her the previous night.

He paused inside the door, his gaze raking over her. "Good God, don't you have anything else to wear that doesn't come out of Camelot?"

Ysabel looked down at her midnight-blue velvet gown that differed only in color from the ivory-colored one she had worn before. "No."

"There's got to be something." He strode over to the closet and searched through the garments hanging in there. "I can't believe this. They're all alike."

"I told you."

"You dressed like this for him all the time?"

"It's what he wanted."

"And you always gave him exactly what he wanted."

"Yes."

"Didn't you look a bit weird when you paid a visit to the local supermarket?"

"I didn't go to town much. I have a few day dresses. They're at the back."

He flipped through the clothes until he found them. "Same style, shorter length."

"It's what he wanted," she repeated. She clasped her hands tightly on her lap. "If you're through prying, can we get on with our discussion?"

"By all means." He shut the closet door and leaned back against it. "Townsend said you wanted a favor."

"Actually, more of a bargain than a favor. I'm willing to compensate you."

"And you have the means to do it now. Camelot pays very well, doesn't it?"

Her hands tightened in her lap. "Yes, very well. May I go on?" She didn't wait for a replay. "Due to your profession you have many contacts in Latin America. Two years ago you did a three-part story on the dictatorship in San Miguel."

"So?"

"It was exceptionally in-depth, so in-depth it angered General Marino enough to cause him to expel you from the country. To obtain that kind of information you must have had very well-placed sources."

He gazed at her, waiting.

"I left something behind when I married Arnold and came here. I want you to help me get it back."

"What?"

She glanced away from him. "Something very valuable to me."

"And you're not going to tell me what it is? How do you expect me to locate this mysterious object?"

"I'll tell you what it is after we've arrived in San Miguel."

He went still. "You want me to actually take you to San Miguel?"

"It's necessary. Your contacts may not be able to find it without help. I know General Marino was upset about the story you did but—"

"I had to hide out in the jungle for two days while Marino's elite guard searched for me before I made my rendezvous with the cruiser that took me off the island. Marino threatened to stake me to an anthill if I ever showed my face in San Miguel again."

"This would be different. You might not even have to be in touch with anyone in the government."

"Might not? That's a little too vague for my peace of mind."

"I can't promise you that it won't be dangerous, but I'll do everything possible to make sure you're not hurt," she said earnestly.

His brows raised. "*You're* supposed to protect me?"

"Yes, I'll protect you."

He started to chuckle and then stopped as he saw her grave expression. "I prefer to protect myself and fervently believe in caution over valor."

"The danger didn't seem to bother you in San Miguel."

"It bothered me. I'm no fool and I like living as well as the next man."

"But your story was worth the risk?"

"It must have been or I wouldn't have hung on until I got it."

A thoughtful frown knitted her brow. "Then all I have to do is to offer you something worth your trouble."

"All?"

"Mr. Townsend said you had something in mind when he told you I needed a favor. What is it?"

"You'd have to offer to spin straw into gold to get me to go back to San Miguel."

"Straw into . . . oh, Rumpelstiltskin." She moistened her lips. "I can't do that but I'll give you anything else."

"Even half of your kingdom?"

"You're talking about the inheritance? You can have it all." She leaned forward and spoke eagerly, "I'll have Mr. Townsend draw up the papers. The moment I have what I want and we leave San Miguel, Winter Castle belongs to you."

He gazed at her in astonishment. "You'd give it up?"

"I don't want it. I never wanted any of it. You can have it all. Just take me to San Miguel."

He was silent a moment, studying her. "I think you mean it."

"Of course, I mean it." She gestured impatiently. "Will you take the island and the castle? You grew up here. The castle must mean something to you."

"And it means nothing to you?"

"Nothing."

"But the money does mean something to you?"

"If it will get me what I want."

"San Miguel." His expression was suddenly intent. "Curioser and curioser."

"Will you take it?" she asked again.

He shook his head. "This place has no fond memories for me."

Disappointment surged through her. "Then why did you come? What do you want?"

He paused for an instant before asking softly, "Haven't you guessed? I want what my father wanted. 'The Winter Bride.'"

"Then take it," she said quickly. "And I'll throw in the island. I'll sign the papers tomorrow."

"Not so fast." He held up his hand. "I'm not sure the painting is worth the price you're asking me to pay. I'll have to make a few phone calls to San Miguel and see how badly Marino still wants my head and if my contacts are still in place."

"How long will that take?"

"A few days, perhaps a week."

She mustn't be impatient, she told herself. A week wasn't so long after seven years. "And you'll contact me when you've made a decision?"

"Oh, before that. I want you to come to the cottage tomorrow afternoon."

She frowned, puzzled. "Why?"

"Call it a whim." He smiled mockingly. "Maybe I just want to look at you. It's not every day I get the opportunity of studying the Winter Bride at close range. You'll indulge me, I trust?"

"I don't see . . ." She trailed off as she met his gaze. His eyes were glittering with mockery and yet she was conscious of something deeper, beneath the surface. Anger? Whatever it was, she must placate him. He *had* to take her to San Miguel. "Yes, I'll come."

"I thought you would. We've already noted how compliant you can be, if it suits you." He moved toward the door. "I'll expect you at three."

Three

Ysabel took a deep breath before knocking on the door of the cottage.

"Come in."

Jed was standing by an ancient black iron cookstove and looked up as she came inside. His brows raised as his gaze took in her long-sleeved ivory jersey chemise and the soft suede of her knee-length off-white boots.

"Ah, I see we have the supermarket Camelot version today."

"My other gowns seemed to annoy you."

"So you decided to mollify me? What a peace-loving nature you have."

"It seemed foolish to let unimportant details get in the way of what is important," she said quietly.

"How sensible." He picked up the dark blue metal coffeepot. "Coffee?"

"No, thank you."

"Sit down. You don't mind if I have some?"

She shook her head before moving across the room to sit down at the table. She glanced around. There wasn't much to see; besides the stove and an equally ancient refrigerator, there were only an oak table and two chairs, bookshelves affixed with brackets to the far wall, a double bed stripped of its linen. The wall opposite her was dominated by a large uncurtained window overlooking the sea and a pine-paneled window seat. The cottage appeared sparkling clean but extremely Spartan. "You can't be very comfortable here. You don't even have bed linens. Why don't you come to the castle?"

"I'm touched by your concern. I tossed out the mattress and sheets when I found they were flea-ridden. I picked up some bedding in town this morning, but I haven't bothered to put it on yet." He poured coffee into a brown mug and then crossed to sit down opposite her at the table. "And I prefer to be on my own."

"Why?"

"I know this will astonish you since I've shown you such a sunny side of my nature, but I was never able to charm your lovable housekeeper. She'd probably strew my bed with thorns tipped with curare." He lifted his cup to his lips. "Besides, I feel at home here. I built this cabin myself when I was a sophomore in college."

"You did?" She looked around with fresh interest. "You appear to have done an amazingly good job of it. A hobby?"

"Partly. I've always liked building things, but at the time I needed a project to ease my frustrations."

She said slowly, "I can understand that."

"Can you?" He leaned back in his chair and regarded her curiously. "And what do you do to ease your frustrations, Ysabel?"

His intonation had become subtly sensual, and she felt heat sting her cheeks. She quickly looked down at her hands folded on the table. "I study."

"What do you study?"

"Everything and anything. I hadn't completed even my secondary education when I married Arnold. I took correspondence courses to get my diploma and then started university courses. I received a bachelor's degree in liberal arts last year."

"It must have been a long and laborious process. Why didn't you go to classes on the mainland?"

"Arnold didn't want me to leave the island."

"Not even to complete your education?"

She kept her voice carefully neutral. "He saw no value in my having any more schooling. However, he did permit me to take the correspondence work to amuse me."

"Permit." He muttered something beneath his breath that sounded obscene. "How generous of him. As long as it didn't interfere with your primary function."

"That's correct." She could feel his intent gaze on her face and tried to change the subject. "There's no telephone here. How will you make your calls to San Miguel?"

"I've already made them. When I went over to the mainland this morning."

"Why didn't you tell me at once?" Her gaze flew to his face. "What did you find out?"

"That Marino still hates my entrails."

"And your contacts?"

"Still in place."

Her clasped hands tightened until the knuckles turned white. "And your decision?"

"I don't have one yet."

"When will you make—"

"I have no idea," he interrupted. "I'm going to have to weigh the advantages and risks. I'll let you know when I do."

She frowned anxiously as she searched his impassive face. "You're not toying with me?"

He smiled mockingly. "You're not very trusting."

"Arnold would sometimes—" She stopped. "No, I guess I'm not."

His smile faded. "I'd forgotten that dirty trick of my father. Hold out a teasing carrot until he got what he wanted and then suddenly the carrot would disappear." His tone harshened. "I don't play those games. I'm not my father, Ysabel."

"But I don't know that, do I? You have some of the same qualities. You like to have your own way and you feel the same about 'The Winter Bride.'"

"Not quite the same. I never built my life around a painting."

"But you still want it."

"Hell yes, I want it. I grew up thinking it would belong to me, and I felt damned cheated when I had to leave it with that bastard. When I was a boy, my mother told me over and over 'The Winter Bride' was *mine.*"

"Why did she do that? She must have known Arnold would never give it up to anyone."

"The island and castle as well as the painting had belonged to her family for over a century."

Her eyes widened in surprise. "I didn't know that. Arnold never mentioned to me how he had acquired the island."

"Oh, he made it very much his own after he married my mother. He had a king complex, and the marriage was the ideal setting for him. He fell in love with the castle and the painting and managed to tolerate my mother until her death"—his lips twisted bitterly—"though he made her life a hell on earth with his affairs and humiliating treatment of her."

And his son's life equally miserable, Ysabel thought with compassion. She had lived in that hell herself for seven long years, but Jed's imprisonment had been for much longer. She impulsively reached across the table and touched his hand. "I'm sorry."

She felt the muscles tense beneath her touch, but he didn't move his hand away. "Don't be. I got over being sorry for myself by the time I was thirteen. After that, I was only angry and set out to make as much trouble for the bastard as I could." He sipped his coffee. "As Townsend will tell you, I got pretty good at it."

"Didn't that hurt your mother too?"

"She was too crushed and broken by then to care. He had gotten her to sign over the castle and 'The Winter Bride' to him, and she lived in an emotional vacuum, scurrying to obey his every wish. Sometimes I caught an expression on her face. . . . I think she was glad I was giving him grief. She was too weak to fight him herself." A sudden edge entered his voice. "Too 'compliant.'"

She became aware of that now familiar scorching wave of feeling reaching out to her, enfolding her. She quickly pulled back her hand. "Then I pity her very much."

"So did I." He leaned forward, his expression granite-hard. "She went into the trap blindly because she thought she loved him. But you knew exactly what you were doing, didn't you?"

"Yes," she answered. "Exactly."

"Then don't expect me to feel the same sympathy for you. We usually reap what we sow."

"I don't expect you to feel anything for me."

"But I *do*, dammit." His voice was thick with frustration. "I feel angry and confused." He paused. "And horny as hell."

She stiffened as shock electrified her.

He smiled grimly. "You're surprised. Why? You told me my father and I are alike in some ways. This is obviously one of them."

The air in the room seemed to have been sucked out. She couldn't breathe. She couldn't do anything but look at him.

"I worked until I was exhausted last night to make sure I'd be able to sleep," he said. "It didn't do any good. I lay there thinking about you and hurting, aching."

"It's not . . . You were upset. It's not me."

"You think it's the Winter Bride?" He shrugged. "Maybe." His voice deepened to silky softness. "Or maybe it's Ysabel."

She shook her head. "It couldn't be . . . We just met."

"Lust at first sight?"

"It has to be the Winter Bride." She moistened her lips. "Coming back here after all these years must be traumatic for you. I'm sure you'll change your mind once you get over the first effects."

"I am over the first shock. You'll find I recover my equilibrium fairly quickly." He reached out and took her hand.

Why hadn't she felt this same sense of tingling awareness when she had touched him before? Heat seemed to be spreading up her arm, and, inexplicably, her breasts were swelling, pushing against the soft jersey of her dress. She instinctively tried to break his hold, but he quickly tightened his grasp.

"No, not yet. I want to touch you." His voice hoarsened as his thumb ran up and down her inner wrist in an erotic caress. "Lord, your skin feels . . ."

"Let me go," she whispered.

He didn't seem to hear her. "That was one of the things I kept thinking about last night. How your cheek felt under my finger as I stroked it. How soft you felt as you lay on the floor under me and how—"

She wrenched her arm away from him and jumped to her feet. "I'd better get back to the castle. Betty will miss me."

"Sit back down. We haven't finished."

She stood looking at him, her hands clenched at her sides.

"You came here so I could look at you at close range," he said softly. "Remember?"

"You've already looked at me."

"Not half as intimately as I'd like to. Not the way I fantasized last night. Would you like me to tell you exactly how I'd like to see you?"

"No." Her voice was shaking and she steadied it. "I'd like to go now please."

"Such submissive politeness. He taught you well, didn't he?" His voice was still soft, but now the tone held a savagery that caused her to step back. "I wonder what else he taught you?"

"May I go now?"

He gazed at her, his eyes glittering in his taut face. Then he gestured wearily toward the door. "Lord, you look like a scared little girl. Get out of here."

She started for the door.

"But come back tomorrow."

She opened the door.

His mocking question followed her. "Well, are you coming back?"

She stood without moving, not looking at him. "You know I'll have to come back. You haven't given me your decision yet."

"Oh yes, San Miguel. How could I forget San Miguel? I'll have to consider my options while I'm waiting for you to come back to me, won't I?"

She didn't answer and the next moment the door closed behind her. She stood there, letting the crisp autumn wind cool her heated cheeks. She was shaking, she noticed without surprise. Those last few moments in the cottage had thrown her into a panic, had destroyed her hard-won serenity. It was only because he had caught her off guard, she assured herself. She had known he felt resentment and anger, but the fact that he also wanted her had shocked her.

Shocked, but not repulsed. Strange how she had not been repulsed as she had felt whenever Arnold had touched her. Sexual chemistry? The thought was as shocking as her response had been. She had never experienced anything approaching the intense physical reaction Jed had stirred in her a few moments ago. She had thought she was one of those women incapable of sexual desire.

She *wouldn't* feel lust for Jed Corbin. Dear heaven, she had seen enough of that emotion on San Miguel to realize what a trap it was for women. She had a purpose to accomplish and nothing must distract her, not when she was so close to her goal. She instinctively knew there was nothing to fear physically in Jed. He was not a man who would use force on a woman, and by the time she saw him tomorrow he would probably have changed his mind about wanting her anyway.

She carefully didn't address the problem of what she would do if he didn't change his mind.

She started up the path away from the cottage, her hurried pace closely resembling flight.

"Come in."

Jed didn't look up from his computer when Ysabel walked into the cottage the following afternoon. "Sit down," he said absently. "I'll be with you in a minute." He went back to whatever he was working on.

So much for her apprehensions and the sleepless night she had spent, Ysabel thought with rueful relief. She had been right in her surmise that his attitude would be different that day.

She closed the door, moved quietly to the window seat, and curled up on the hard wood, gazing out at the sea. She had always loved the sea in all its moods. She concentrated, closing out both the sound of Jed's typing and her own nervousness.

She was still sitting in the same position two hours later when she became conscious the typing had stopped.

"What are you thinking about?"

She shifted her gaze to his face. "I beg your pardon?"

"I've been rude enough to make you sit there for hours and you still look as contented as a hand fed Siamese cat." He leaned back in his chair. "Daydreaming?"

"I . . . suppose."

"Don't you know? Or don't you want to share it with me?"

"I don't . . . I've always . . . Why are you interested?"

"I'm interested because you weren't on the same planet with me." His voice had a definite edge. "It . . . bothers me."

"Why? Arnold never . . ." She stopped as she saw the flicker of anger in his expression.

"I'm not my father. In many ways I'm a hell of a lot more demanding. I'm not content with a costumed figurine."

"You're not being reasonable." She laughed tremulously. "You said you only wanted to look at me. What difference does it make what I'm thinking?"

"It makes a difference. I want to know . . ." He trailed off in frustration. "First, I kept you waiting, then I start to pry and bully you, and you just sit there cool and controlled and let me do it. Why don't you tell me to go to hell?"

"I don't want to make you angry," she said simply.

He muttered something beneath his breath, and his chair screeched back as he rose to his feet.

She flinched, stiffening warily as he came toward her.

He stopped in his tracks as he saw her expression. "For Lord's sake, I'm not going to hit you." A sudden thought occurred to him. "Did he ever strike you?"

She didn't answer.

"Did he?"

She could see he wasn't going to give up. "Not often."

"Not often," he repeated, stunned.

"Only at the beginning," she went on quickly. "Before I learned how to please him."

"He actually struck you?" he asked thickly. "My God, the last time I saw him he weighed over two hundred pounds and you weren't much more than a child. He was a tyrant with women, but he never physically abused them."

"Our relationship was different."

"Because he knew you wouldn't fight back." His eyes were suddenly blazing. "Why didn't you fight him, dammit?"

"It wasn't in our agreement. I promised . . ."

"What did you promise?"

"To do anything, be anything he wanted me to be," she whispered.

"Even his punching bag?"

"It didn't happen often."

"It shouldn't have happened at all." His hands grasped her shoulders and tightened with unconscious cruelty. "I want to shake you. How could you let him—" He drew a deep breath, his expression filled with self-disgust when her face contorted with pain. "And now I'm doing it." He released her shoulders. "Like father, like son. And would you let me beat you too?"

"You're not like him."

"That's not the question. Would you let me abuse you, if I liked?"

"Yes," she said clearly.

He looked as if she had struck him. "Lord."

"Did you think I'd say no?" Her voice was suddenly fierce, her eyes blazing at him. "Pain is *nothing*. I can endure anything, do anything I have to do."

"For money?"

"Money is only a means to an end."

"For San Miguel?"

She drew a steadying breath. "I told you I had to go back. Nothing is more important than that."

He gazed at her for a moment, then turned on his heel, strode across the room and dropped into his chair. "Then you'll have to find someone else to take you."

"I didn't choose you randomly. After I ran across that magazine article about how you got the San Miguel story, I dug out everything about you that I could. I researched and I thought a long time before I decided you were the best man to help me."

He shook his head. "You're wrong. I'm the worst choice you could make." He reached out and grasped the edge of the table. "You have a very weird effect on me. I can't be in the same room with you for three minutes without being thrown into turmoil."

"Yet you worked for two hours today and entirely forgot my presence."

"Not entirely. I could *feel* you there. I just didn't acknowledge you."

"Then all you have to do is continue to close me out."

"It's not that easy. Whenever I'm around you, I find myself reverting to that undisciplined hellion I was fourteen years ago." He smiled bitterly. "I give you fair warning. I don't react either sensibly or logically to you."

"All right, I can accept that."

"You can accept anything, right? You can take that bastard's lust and abuse. You can let him—" He broke off. "You see? I'm out of control where you're concerned. Better get away from me while you still can."

She shook her head.

He suddenly smiled recklessly. "Then on your head be it. Why should I worry about you? You know what you want and what you're willing to do to get it. From now on I'll just sit back and enjoy the benefits of being the chosen one of our meek little Winter Bride."

"I'm not meek."

"No, you're something a good deal more interesting and challenging." He placed his knee on the table and leaned back, causing his chair to teeter on its back legs. His demeanor had changed and had become coolly, almost insolently, confident. "I think we'll test that philosophy of acceptance in the next few days. I want to see just how much you want me to go to San Miguel."

"I've told you—"

"But I've always believed actions speak louder than words."

"What do you want from me?"

"That you come here tomorrow and the day after tomorrow and the day after that. I want you to obey me as you did my father and 'accept' anything I ask of you."

"And will you take me to San Miguel, if I do?"

"No promises." His tone was hard. "I have no intention of making it easy for you. At the end of that time I'll make a decision and it may very well be no." He paused. "And the only thing you may have accomplished is pleasing me. You'd be a fool to agree."

She searched his face and saw something there that caused her eyes to widen with wonder. "You want me to refuse."

"Do I? That would be foolish of me."

She frowned. "You're a very perplexing man. I don't understand you."

"Yes or no?"

She hesitated but there was only one possible answer. "I'll do as you wish, of course."

The front legs of the chair came down on the floor. "Great." His savage tone did not reflect the sentiment. "Be here at eleven o'clock tomorrow morning."

"How long will I have to stay?"

"Until I tell you to go."

"A few hours are no problem but if I'm gone too long, Betty may prove difficult."

"Good Lord, does she order you about too? She's your housekeeper, not your warden." He added roughly, "Tell the shrew to mind her own business."

It was easier said than done, she thought. He had no conception how hard it had been for her to escape Betty's eagle eye for the last two days. "I'll be here at eleven." She started across the room.

He caught her arm as she passed his chair. "Wait."

She stood still, bracing herself.

"Easy." His voice was hoarse, his tone halting. "I just wanted to . . ." His head lowered and his lips gently pressed against the flesh of her inner wrist. "I'm sorry I hurt you." Then her hand was free. "Eleven o'clock," he said gruffly, not looking at her.

Tenderness. She could not equate the emotion with Jed, but there was no denying the exquisite tenderness of that kiss. She stared down at his thick silver hair and felt a sudden urge to reach out and touch it, smooth it, comb her fingers through the wiry, curly mop. The impulse was as bewildering as his action had been and frightened her more than anything that had happened that day.

"Good-bye," she muttered and fled.

Four

"It's almost dark. I'd like to go back to the castle now."

"What? No please?" he asked mockingly as he looked up from his computer. "Where are those elegant geisha girl manners? Careful or they'll expel you from the union."

She tried to smother the sudden flash of pain that shot through her at his words. She had never known anyone who could so effortlessly destroy her self-control. She had sat calmly while Arnold had verbally torn her to pieces, but Jed's sarcasm touched a strange, hurtful chord. "Please," she said. "I thought my politeness annoyed you."

"Everything about you annoys me. The way you look at me, the way you don't look at me, that soft, husky voice." He turned off the computer. "This garbage I've been writing all afternoon."

"You can't blame me for your lack of creativity. I

haven't made you . . . You haven't said two words to me since I arrived here."

"That doesn't mean I've not been aware of you." He scowled moodily. "You've played hell with my concentration."

She had known he had been as aware of her as she had been of him. For the past six hours she had sat there in the window seat, every muscle locked with the tension that vibrated like a live electric wire between them. She looked down at her hands folded on her lap. "That's hardly my fault either. It's not my choice to be here. If you wanted to work, it would have been more sensible to let me stay at the castle."

"I didn't want to work. I wanted to see if I could—look at me, dammit." When her gaze lifted to meet his, he said, "I don't like not being in control. I thought I could shut you out, but it's not working anymore."

"I haven't done anything to disturb you."

"Which disturbs me more than anything you could do. You sit there with your hands folded and your expression as serene as a Madonna's and I want to break something. I want to break *you*." He got up and moved slowly toward her. "I want to hear you yell at me and pound me. I want to see you without that blasted armor."

He was now so close, she could see the pupils of his glittering eyes and feel the heat of his body reaching out and enfolding her. She couldn't breathe. "I don't know what you mean. I have no armor."

"The hell you haven't." He reached out and trailed his index finger down her throat, leaving a path of fire in its wake. "But any armor can be pierced with the right weapon." His thumb settled in the hollow of her throat, testing the tempo of her heart. "You like my touching you?"

Like was not the word, she thought in bewilderment. His touch was arousing a pleasure so excruciatingly intense, it was close to pain.

"Let's see what else you like." His head slowly lowered as his hand moved down to cup her breast. "Open your mouth."

Her breast was swelling, the nipple hardening, and she felt a clenching of the muscles of her stomach.

"Open," he repeated softly.

She closed her eyes and obeyed him.

His tongue . . .

She heard him groan low in his throat as his fingers opened and closed on her breast. "More." His tongue ravaged, teased, played, sank deep. Then his other hand was behind her, unzipping the long zipper at the back of her dress. "Give me more."

The dress was down at her waist, and her undergarments had somehow come off too. . . .

He lifted her so that she was kneeling on the window seat. His mouth hovered and then enveloped her breast.

She gasped as she felt the strong sucking pressure. She swayed forward, her hands grasping blindly for his shoulders. His mouth switched to the other breast, while his hand wandered over her stomach, curved around and cupped her buttocks. She heard herself making tiny sounds that were somewhere between a whimper and a groan as his palms opened and closed on her bottom.

He lifted his head. His cheeks were flushed, his eyes brilliant, his lips heavy with sensuality. With shaking hands he pushed the dress down and lifted her out of it. "Beautiful . . ." He threw the dress aside. He ran his fingers through her hair until it was a wild, tousled mop. "I think we'll leave the boots on. I've always liked the feel of suede against my skin." His tongue licked delicately at her nipple as his hand moved slowly, sensuously back and forth over the instep of the boot. "Tough and yet velvet soft." His hand left the boot and moved up to pet the curls surrounding her womanhood. "Like this. But this is going to feel even better against me. Soft, springy . . ."

His words were almost as erotic as his touch, and the sight of his long tanned fingers on her body sent a hot shudder through her. What was happening to her? She was melting, mindless, her hips lifting to his hand as if begging for more.

"You like it?" he muttered, tugging at the curls. "It's going to be hard to wait, isn't it? Lie down, love." He pushed her back on the window seat, parting her thighs and then standing back to look at her. "Lord, I want you."

She could see his bold arousal changing the shape of his jeans, his nostrils flaring as he looked down at her. It was strange lying there totally exposed before him, the sun streaming through the window, warm on her naked skin, the pine window seat hard beneath her buttocks.

His hand cupped her womanhood, his fingers teasing, searching. "Tell me you want me."

"I . . . do."

His finger entered her, probed, played. "Say the words."

She arched upward with a cry of sheer need.

He laughed hoarsely. "That was very satisfactory but I want more. Tell me you like it."

"Yes." She was dizzy, whirling, writhing with heat and need. "Jed . . ."

"I like the sound of that too." His lips enveloped her breast again, his finger stroking her. "Say my name again."

She looked down at his silver head nestled against her breast, his teeth tugging at her nipple. The ache between her thighs was growing until she could think of nothing else. "Jed?"

"You want an end to it? I do too." He delicately licked her. "Just tell me you want me too. I need to know."

He must be able to see how he was making her feel, she thought wildly. She couldn't stand much more of this. "I . . . want you to do anything you want to do." Surely that would be enough.

He stiffened against her. "Those words sound vaguely familiar." He lifted his head to look at her grimly. "Are you by any chance 'accepting' me, Ysabel?"

She was too bewildered by the change in him to answer and his anger flared. "Damn you," he said softly. He straightened away from her. "Get the hell out of here."

She looked up at him dazedly. "You want me to leave?"

"No, I want you over on that bed, moving underneath me," he said harshly. "And if you don't get out of here in the next minute that's just where you'll be. Get moving."

She sat up and reached for her dress. It was difficult to move when her body felt so heavy and yet erotically sensitive.

"Too slow." He snatched up her dress, slipped it over her head, and pulled it down over her body. Then he jerked her to her feet and pushed her toward the door. "Go on. Run back and hide out in that turreted cocoon."

She was still too shaken to fully understand him. "You don't want me to come back tomorrow?"

"You're damned right I want you back here," he said grimly. "By then I'll have had time to get over these inconvenient twinges of consciousness and be able to take what I want." He turned his back on her, every muscle rigid. "Get out of here."

She ran out of the cottage and kept on running until she reached the castle. She felt on fire, her skin flushed and feverish. What had happened to her? she wondered desperately as she went into the foyer and started up the stone steps. She would not go back tomorrow. What he made her feel was too dangerous and she couldn't let herself be swept away. Perhaps she could find some other way to—

"What are you up to, Ysabel? I saw you flying up the path like the devil was after you."

Ysabel froze and looked at Betty standing at the foot of the stairs. She suddenly became conscious of her windblown hair, and scorching heat climbed to her cheeks as she realized she was not wearing anything beneath her dress. Her unbound breasts, outlined against the silky material, seemed terribly betraying. She felt almost as if Betty must be able to see what had happened at the cottage. She quickly turned her back to the housekeeper. "N-nothing's wrong," she stammered. "I just felt like running."

"Mr. Arnold wouldn't like it. He always wanted you to move with dignity."

"I forgot."

"You seem to be forgetting too much of what we taught you." Betty's voice sharpened. "Where have you been all day?"

"I took a long walk."

"You've been taking a lot of walks lately."

Ysabel's patience nearly snapped. Dear heaven, she couldn't cope with Betty's suspicions in her present state. She wanted to explode, to rant and rave and strike out. "Walks are good for me." She added deliberately, "Just like hot chocolate."

"Are you being insolent?"

"I'm merely stating a fact." Before Betty could reply she ran up the steps and out of sight.

But not out of earshot. She heard the housekeeper's curse and shuddered at the venom in the woman's voice. She was accustomed to Betty's poisonous nature, but still it sickened her. How could the woman derive such pleasure from the unhappiness she inflicted?

She knew the answer. Power. Why else had Betty willingly lived and thrived in Arnold's dark shadow all these years if they hadn't been addicted to the same vice?

Ysabel slammed the door of her room, desperately hoping Betty wouldn't follow her. Her control was almost gone and she didn't know if she could keep herself from lashing out. *Damn* the woman! She wanted to send something crashing against the far wall as she had done in those early days before she had learned to mask the anger and frustration within her.

She waited. No heavy footsteps in the hall, she realized with relief. Evidently she was going to be spared the usual tirade. She moved quickly to the shower, shedding her clothes along the way.

Her breasts still felt full, achy, and the water spraying them brought back the memory of Jed's silver head bent over her, his hot mouth sucking. . . . Sweet mercy, her nipples were hardening at the thought, and the throbbing emptiness between her thighs was becoming painful.

She mustn't remember how she had responded to Jed in those moments on the window seat. She had known from that first day at the cabin that the payment Jed might demand was sexual, and had come to terms with it. But she hadn't dreamed her own feelings would become involved. Yet was it so wicked that her body had enjoyed what he did to her? She had read that many people could compartmentalize their feelings and perhaps if she concentrated on that she could . . .

What was she thinking? Through desperation and necessity she had learned at moments of stress to withdraw into her own world, but she had never learned to completely shut away hurt.

She would just have to adjust to the situation. From Jed's last words it was clear he still had every intention of taking her to bed. If that was to happen, then she must find a way to gain and not lose from the experience.

A child. The thought came like a ray of sunlight. She had always loved children and desperately wanted one of her own but thought she would never have one because she couldn't bear to be touched. Since Jed had managed to break through that barrier, wasn't a child a possibility now? A rush of warm contentment went through her at the thought. Yes, she could give Jed what he wanted of her and take something infinitely more precious in return.

A child of her own.

He stood in the middle of the room and she inhaled sharply as she looked at him. It was as if she were staring into the heart of a storm; she could almost feel the swirling turbulence of emotion around him.

"You're late," he said hoarsely. "I didn't think you were coming."

"I had to wait until Betty—What are—"

"Hush." He had scooped her up in his arms and was carrying her toward the bed. His face was so close, she could see the dark shadows beneath his eyes, the lines of strain engraved beside his lips. "Don't say anything." He put her down on the bed and stood over her, his hands clenched. "Unless it's no, and then you'd better say it loud, clear, and fast." He waited for only an instant and began unbuttoning his shirt. "Then, let's get on with it before I go crazy. Lord, I'm hurting."

She was hurting too. Every breath was painful and her skin felt hot, tingling as if the nerve endings were vibrating. "Should I be doing some-thing?"

"The usual." He was stripping swiftly. "Undress."

She pulled the chemise over her head and tossed it on the floor. "The boots?"

He straightened, his gaze wandering over her. "You obviously came prepared."

"It seemed foolish to wear anything beneath the dress when you said you intended—" She stopped, looking at him. Muscular power and masculine arousal. She had never known how beautiful that combination could be until that moment. She moistened her lips. "Should I take off the boots this time?"

"I'll take them off," he said thickly. "Right foot."

She extended it and he slipped one hand be-neath her knee while the other cupped the heel of the suede boot. "I understand the back of the knee is supposed to be an erogenous zone." He gently massaged the soft flesh as he worked the boot off her foot. "Is it?"

A tingling was starting to spread up her thigh. "I think . . . so."

He tossed the boot aside and cupped her instep, his thumb running lightly over the sole of her foot. "And here?"

The tingling again; her calf went rigid.

"I see it is." He put down her foot and stood there, looking down at her, his face contorted as if he were in pain. "After you left yesterday, I called myself all kinds of fool. I was hurting so bad, I almost followed you to the castle. I didn't give a damn if you were only 'accepting' me. Then I thought 'No, gain control. Don't let her do this to you. Wait. Treat her like any other woman.'" He jerked off the other boot, parted her thighs, and moved between them. "It's just sex. Foreplay and then . . ." He laughed harshly as he took her hand and put it over his heart. "Foreplay? Feel me. I've barely touched you and I'm about to have a heart attack."

She experienced a primitive sense of satisfaction as she felt the rapid thunder beneath her palm. "I like it. It makes me feel . . ."

"Power?" His hand cupped her, and he watched as she arched up off the bed at his touch. "Pleasure?"

"Yes," she whispered.

He was nudging against her. "No foreplay. I can't take any more. I don't care if you want me, will you take me?"

"I do want you. I do—"

She smothered a cry as he drove into the heart of her!

He froze above her. "Ysabel?"

Full and yet still empty. Her breath was coming in little pants as she held on to his shoulders. "It's all right. The pain's gone. I want . . ." She moved yearningly, trying to take more, and felt a shudder go through him. "Please."

"I'm afraid I'll hurt you. You're too tight. . . ."

"Please."

"Lord, don't—" He exploded, driving, rotating. Pleasure. Heat. Need.

She found herself whimpering, lifting her hips to meet every thrust, her nails biting into his shoulders as she tried to get closer, to take more of him.

"Easy." His lips grazed her forehead. "Slow."

She couldn't; the tempo was too intense, the pleasure too heady, the tension building too quickly. "More . . . please."

He chuckled. "I'm beginning to like that word." He turned over so that she was astride him. "All right, hold on, love."

The next moments were as wild as being caught in a whirlwind. He bucked, moved her, bucked again. Fast, slow, hard, easy, riding the currents, fighting the currents, and all the time the tension growing.

He turned her over again, his hands digging in her hair as he drove deep. His face was twisted, his breath labored. "Ysabel . . ."

How beautiful her name sounded on his lips, like a clear velvet chord . . .

The tension broke, splintering, engulfing her.

From somewhere far away, she heard him groan and then he arched his back, his eyes closed. He collapsed on top of her, shuddering.

"Dear Lord," he muttered.

She was shaking, too, she realized dazedly. "I feel . . . very weak. Is that a normal reaction?"

"Nothing about this was normal." His breath was still labored. "It was . . . mind-boggling." He paused. "Including the fact that you didn't have the experience to know what was normal and what wasn't." He got off her and sat up. "As I'm aware my father wasn't into platonic relationships and was as lusty as a bull, I'd be interested to have an explanation for this phenomenon."

She didn't look at him. "Arnold knew he was impotent before our marriage. He had contracted some kind of disease that—"

"No wonder he kept you prisoner here. He wanted to make sure no other man grazed where he couldn't." He reached out and possessively cupped her breast in his hand. "I'm not sure I wouldn't feel the same way. It must have driven him crazy to know you could respond like this and not be able to take advantage of it."

"I wasn't . . . he thought I was cold."

His eyes widened. "You? Lord, I've never known a woman so responsive."

"It was different with you."

"Well, you definitely did more than 'accept' me." His eyes narrowed on her face. "Under the circumstances I find that a little unusual. Why?"

"You wanted it."

He muttered an oath. "No, dammit, it was more than that."

"You had your reasons and I had mine. I didn't ask why you wanted me. I don't care if it was because you only wanted to make love to the Winter Bride." That wasn't true, but he must not know how inexplicably painful she found the thought.

"I told you I wasn't my father," he said harshly. "'The Winter Bride' has nothing to do with what happened here today."

"I don't believe you." She met his gaze. "And yes, I had my own reason for coming to your bed, but I have no intention of sharing it with you."

"And lust has nothing to do with it?"

"Oh yes, I told you I wanted you." She smiled tremulously. "It came as a great surprise to me."

He suddenly went still. "How much of a surprise? I assumed you were protected, but I—"

"Don't worry about it."

"You're on the Pill?"

"Isn't every woman these days?" she asked evasively.

"Not if her husband is impotent."

"Arnold never wanted to admit his affliction wasn't only temporary." At least, that was the truth.

He relaxed. "I couldn't be happier that he was wrong." An expression of sensual satisfaction crossed his face. "You were so tight, I felt as if I were a part of you. It was like nothing . . . Good Lord, you're *blushing.*"

Her hand flew to her cheek. "It's an unusual situation for me. I'm a little . . . unsure."

His gaze searched her face. "And where did all that infuriating serenity go?"

"I have to work at it and you're disturbing me. Will you please remove your hand?"

"I like it here." He gently squeezed her breast and watched with bemusement as it began to swell in his grasp. "I think you like it too."

"It makes me . . ." She moistened her lips. "I believe you're very good at this."

"Thank you," he said solemnly. "A man always likes to hear he's been adequate to the task. Though, taking your inexperience into account, I can't consider you an authority on the subject."

She tilted her head. "You're laughing. I've never

seen you really laugh before. It seems a very peculiar time for it."

"You're right, this is no time for humor." He moved over her and parted her thighs. "There are very serious doings in the works."

Five

"Slut!"

The word jarred Ysabel from the light doze into which she had fallen.

Her lids flew open to see Betty framed in the doorway, her features twisted in rage. "Whore!" She stomped across the room toward the bed. "Get away from him."

Ysabel instinctively reached out for Jed's hand.

He sat up in bed, leisurely pulling the coverlet over his hips. "I see the years haven't taught you courtesy. It's polite to knock."

Betty ignored him, her cold gray eyes fastened on Ysabel. "Did you think I wouldn't find out you were sneaking down here? Mr. Arnold was always afraid of this. He warned me you'd betray him if you got the chance, that I'd have to watch you every minute." Her gaze turned balefully on Jed. "You had to do it, didn't you? You always hated him and what better way to get your revenge than make a whore of his—"

"Easy, Betty." A steely inflection had entered Jed's voice. "I'm no longer amused. Suppose you get the hell out of this cottage."

"I belong on this island, Mr. Arnold saw to that. You're the intruder." Betty turned back to Ysabel. "Get your clothes on. I'm taking you back to the castle where you belong."

What better way to get your revenge?

The woman's words echoed in Ysabel's mind, bringing with them a mysterious hurt.

Betty glared down at her. "You heard me. What are you waiting for?"

There was no reason to be hurt, Ysabel told herself. She had known Jed's feelings for her were complicated, and revenge was probably one of them.

Betty's hard palm lashed out and connected with her left cheek.

Ysabel's head snapped back as the room went black for an instant. She dimly heard Jed's low exclamation and realized he had exploded into motion.

He was off the bed in one leap, his hand grasping Betty's nape. "Out!" he said between his teeth. "Or you'll find yourself tossed into the ocean and swimming back to the castle."

"Not without her. It's my duty to make sure she—" She squealed as Jed's grip tightened and he forced her toward the door.

"Ysabel, you get up out of that bastard's bed and come along. I don't know what's wrong with you. You know you must obey—"

Her words were cut off as Jed pushed her out of the cottage, slammed and locked the door behind her.

He stood there a moment, his hands clenched at his sides. "Lord, I came close to strangling the old bitch." He strode back to the bed. "Did she hurt you?"

"No," she lied. Her cheek still stung from the blow. She raised a shaky hand to comb back her hair from her face. "I'm fine."

"The hell you are." He tilted up her face, and his fingertips gently traced the bruised flesh. "She really gave you a wallop. It seems my father wasn't the only one who used you for a punching bag."

"Betty's never struck me." She had to force herself to remain stiff and unyielding. His touch was so gentle, she wanted to lean forward into his arms. Dear Heaven, she needed comforting right now. She felt raw and exposed and unable to close out the ugliness. "I guess she's never been this angry before."

"Because you probably always gave in to her." He stood up and moved toward the sink. "And you never slept with the enemy." He took a clean washcloth from a drawer beneath the sink and dampened it with water from the faucet. "Lord, she must be losing her marbles to think she can get away with something like this."

"She's never been very stable where I was concerned. My marriage to Arnold was like salt on an open wound. She was in love with him, you know."

He wheeled to face her. "What?"

"I don't think he ever saw it, but I wasn't on the

island a month before I realized it. When he paid me too much attention, it hurt her."

"And then she made you hurt too."

She nodded.

"Why didn't you tell me she was this much of a threat to you?"

"You wouldn't have understood. I think you saw her as some kind of a joke."

"Well, I don't view her that way any longer." He was beside her, dabbing the cold cloth on the bruise. "This is *not* funny."

"No." She was beginning to shake. She had to get out of there before he noticed. She reached up and covered his hand to stop the soothing motion. "It doesn't hurt anymore. I think I'll get up and get dressed now, if you don't mind."

"If I don't mind? You've just been attacked and you're wondering if I mind if you put your clothes on?" He tossed the washcloth on the floor. "What the hell do you think I am?"

"I'm sorry. I didn't mean to make you angry again. I don't seem to be able to think very—"

"Good Lord, you're shaking yourself to pieces." He sat down on the bed and drew her into his arms. "Relax. You're as stiff as a board."

"This isn't necessary. I'm really quite all right."

"Sure, that's why you're shuddering like a malaria victim. Give in, dammit. I'm not going to hold it against you if you react like a normal person."

She was afraid to give in. She had held on so long, she wasn't sure what would happen if she let down the barriers.

"Fine, let's approach it in a different way." His fingers stroked her hair. "You said you'd accept anything I wanted of you. I'm going to be very upset if you don't stop this nonsense. You don't want me to be upset with you, do you? It would spoil all your plans."

"No I . . . you mustn't . . ." She suddenly collapsed against him, her arms encircling and holding him tightly. "I'm so sorry. . . ."

"Hush." His tone was rough, but the hands stroking her hair was exquisitely gentle. "You're human. It's stupid being sorry you're human." She should push him away, but she couldn't seem to move. She felt as if she were breaking apart inside and all the pieces were flowing into him. "You're just a kid . . . so little." His voice was thick. "Why couldn't they see how damn little you are?"

Peace. Warmth. Strength.

She stayed quite still, cherishing the moments, taking from him. Minutes passed. Finally, reluctantly, she straightened and scooted a few inches away and immediately felt alone. She didn't look at him as she said haltingly, "I thank you very much."

"You're very welcome." He looked at her quizzically. "Okay?"

"Of course. It was only the shock. I wasn't prepared for her." She swung her feet to the floor and jumped out of bed. "I'd better get dressed and get back to the castle."

He stiffened. "The hell you are."

She quickly began to dress.

"You're not going back there," he stated flatly.

"I have to go back. I have nowhere else to go." She sat down and pulled on her boots. "When do you want me to come back?"

"I'm supposed to let you go back and face that six-foot dragon again?"

"She's no danger."

"You have a bruise that will last you a week that says otherwise."

"I told you, she caught me off guard. I'm not afraid of her."

"Well, I'm afraid for you."

She turned to stare at him. "You are?"

"Don't look so surprised. I'm responsible for that she-devil hurting you. It's not going to happen again."

"It won't." She tried to ignore the warmth flowing through her as she smoothed her hair into some semblance of order. "Shall I come back tomorrow?"

"Lord, you're stubborn." His gaze narrowed on her face. "Hasn't it occurred to you that you could use this to force my decision on San Miguel?"

"No." She gave him a faint smile. "I told you I wasn't good at manipulating events to suit myself." She strode toward the door. "And if I tried, you'd probably toss me in the sea like you threatened to do to Betty."

"Let me understand this scenario. You'll just come back here and let me use you until I get tired of it and then go back to the castle and be abused by that Godzilla?" His breath escaped in an exasperated rush. "You're unbelievable."

"I'm sure I'll be—"

"All right, dammit. I'll take you to San Miguel."

She stilled, her heart leaping with joy. "You will?" she whispered. "Truly?"

"I don't lie, Ysabel." He smiled crookedly. "I'll

consider it a catharsis. I take it you're still willing to accept me in your bed?"

"Yes."

"It's a long way to San Miguel. Since you appear to have become an obsession with me, maybe I'll get you out of my system by the time we get there."

"When can we leave?" she asked eagerly. "Right away?"

He nodded curtly. "I want you out of that place."

After all these years it was going to happen. She closed her eyes, dizzy with relief.

"What's wrong? Are you okay?"

Her lids flew open and a brilliant smile lit her face. "Nothing's wrong. Nothing in the world is wrong." She hurried to the door, unlocked it and threw it open. "I'll be back in an hour. I have to pack and get my passport and . . ." She stopped as she remembered something. "Oh dear, my passport's expired."

"I have a few friends in the State Department who can rush a renewal." He started to dress. "Wait for me. I'll go with you."

She shook her head. "Don't bother. Your presence will only complicate things."

"You're not facing that bitch alone."

She glanced at him over her shoulder. "She won't hurt me."

"How do you know?"

"Because I won't let her." Her face was radiant with joy. "Don't you see? It's over!"

She heard him call after her but didn't stop. She felt as if she were floating instead of walking as she climbed the hill toward the castle. She hadn't expected this overpowering euphoria to envelop her, but she welcomed it. It would bolster her strength for the scene that was sure to come with Betty.

"So he sent you packing?" Betty sneered as soon as Ysabel walked in the front door. "It's no more than I expected. Do you know how many women have been in that cottage before you? He was like a tomcat flaunting those sluts he'd bring from the mainland. Every now and then I'd see them parading down the pier back to his boat and think— Where are you going?"

"To my room." Ysabel quickly climbed the steps.

Betty hurried after her, still spurting venom. "He only used you to get back at Mr. Arnold and you let him do it. You spread your legs and let that spawn of Satan—"

"Be quiet, Betty." Ysabel threw open her bedroom door and crossed to the closet.

"Don't you be insolent with me." Betty marched in after her. "You've been too uppity by far since— What are you doing?"

Ysabel pulled out her pigskin suitcase and flung it on the bed. She went to the bureau, gathered up an armful of underwear and carried it to the suitcase.

"Answer me."

"Isn't it evident? I'm packing."

"You're moving into that cottage with him?"

"I'm leaving Winter Island."

Betty gasped. "You can't leave. You belong here."

Ysabel went to the closet and gazed with distaste at the collection of dresses and gowns. She took one dress to wear on the trip, gathered up three pairs of suede boots and carried them to the bed. The soft suede rubbed against her arms as she threw them into the suitcase.

"I've always liked the feel of suede against my skin."

A flash of heat went through her and she paused for a moment, gazing down blindly. Good Heaven, she must be turning into a nymphomaniac if just the thought of him could cause this reaction.

"Ah, you've come to your senses," Betty said with smug satisfaction as she saw Ysabel's slight hesitation. "Now unpack that suitcase and I'll try to forget all this nonsense."

"Go away, Betty." Ysabel turned and went to the desk, opened the top drawer and got out her passport and checkbook. She put the documents in a purse. "I have things to do and you're in my way."

Betty's jaw went slack. "What did you say?"

"You heard me."

"You're actually going?"

"After I shower and change." She moved past Betty as she headed for the bathroom. "I don't want you here when I come out."

Betty's meaty hand closed on Ysabel's arm and jerked her around to face her. "You've forgotten your place, slut. I'll teach you—"

"Let . . . me . . . go." Ysabel spaced the words with icy precision. "You've never taught me anything nor shall you ever. I choose what I will or will not learn. It was my choice that I let you bully me all these years. But all of that is over now. You're a wicked, cruel woman and I hope I never see you again as long as I live."

Betty's hand tightened on her wrist. "You little savage upstart."

"I said, let me go." Her eyes blazed with ferocity, her entire being focused on enforcing her will on the woman. "You're right, I can be savage. I was taught the art in a school you've never attended and I've never forgotten one single lesson."

Betty laughed contemptuously. "You're no bigger than a puppy snapping at my heels."

"It won't make any difference."

"You think you can make me—" Her laughter faded and ceased altogether as she met Ysabel's gaze. She took a step back.

Ysabel pried her fingers off her arm. "Never again, Betty. You will never touch me again." She turned toward the bathroom. "Get out!"

Betty shook herself, trying to regain her aplomb. "You'll be sorry. He doesn't want you. He only wants the Winter Bride just as Mr. Arnold did. When he's tired of you, you'll come running back here to me and—"

"I'll never come back here. I told you, it's over."

She shut the door on Betty's enraged face.

She desperately hoped Betty hadn't seen that she had drawn blood on that parting shot. She was being foolish. What did she care if Jed was obsessed with the blasted painting? No emotional attachment existed between them, only this powerful sensual need. It didn't matter if he saw her only as . . .

It did matter.

Well, she must not let it matter. Her new life was just beginning and she had too much to accomplish to moan and weep about the things she couldn't change.

"Are you okay?" Jed's concerned gaze searched her face as he took her suitcase and then lifted her into the speedboat.

"Fine." She smiled as she sat down beside him. "I told you there would be no problem."

"You seem in excellent spirits anyway. She didn't try to stop you?"

She quickly changed the subject. "Where are we going from here?"

"The airport in Seattle. I'll make a phone call there to a friend in Puerto Rico before we catch a flight out to San Juan. From San Juan we'll go by cabin cruiser to San Miguel."

"Won't going by sea take a long time?"

He shrugged. "About four days but it's safer than by air when you need to enter a country unobtrusively." He started the engine and backed away from the dock. "And I plan on being very unobtrusive, I assure you."

"So do I."

"You couldn't prove it by what you've told me, or I should say *not* told me. Am I allowed to ask how long you think it's going to take to find this treasure you left?"

"I'm not sure. It depends on how good your contacts are."

He slanted her a glance. "And you're not going to confide in me, I take it."

"When we get to San Miguel."

He cast a glance at the suitcase. "You didn't pack much."

"There wasn't anything I wanted to take away from here." She looked out over the water. "As soon as we reach San Miguel, I'll sign over possession of 'The Winter Bride' to you."

"How very cautious of you. No San Miguel, no Bride?"

"I didn't mean . . . I know you wouldn't back out on your promise."

"You don't know anything about me," he said harshly.

"Yes, I do. I know you're tenacious, courageous, and determined. I also know you're intelligent . . . and that you're not as hard as you'd like the world to believe." She smiled. "And I'm learning more all the time."

He studied her face. "This isn't going to be easy. We'll be lucky if we get out of San Miguel with our necks intact."

"It will be all right. Nothing will happen to you."

"I'm glad you're so certain." He shook his head. "You seem damn happy about all this. You're practically glowing."

"Glowing? I feel like I'm blazing inside." She glanced back over her shoulder at the rapidly receding island. "It's starting, Jed!"

Ysabel gazed up at the towering hotel as she got out of the taxi. "I thought we were going directly to the cruiser as soon as we reached San Juan."

"I have to meet someone who's staying here at the hotel."

"Who?"

"Ronnie Dalton, a business associate."

"Is that who you called from the airport at Seattle?"

"Yes, we'll leave tonight if Ronnie's managed to lease the cruiser, but I want to make a few more arrangements."

"Like what?"

"Getting your passport in order before we take off." He tipped the taxi driver, took Ysabel's elbow, and propelled her toward the entrance. "There's no telling where we'll end up before this is over."

"You're truly worried, aren't you? You think we'll run into trouble?"

"I always subscribe to Murphy's Law. Then I'm never disappointed."

"Things aren't going to go wrong this time." She couldn't keep the lilt from her voice as she entered the hotel. "I *feel* it."

"I hope you're right." He gazed concernedly at her radiant face. "Seven years is a long time, Ysabel. A rapine dictatorship like San Miguel's gobbles up everything of value in sight."

"Are you trying to protect me again?" She shot him an amused glance. "Why? You're not—"

"It's about time you got here." A slender, fair-haired young woman dressed in faded jeans and a worn brown leather flight jacket was striding toward them across the lobby. Ysabel received a swift impression of wide-set green eyes, tousled golden curls, and a roses and cream complexion. The rough clothes should have made her appear boyish, but instead she looked like a slightly scruffy angel.

She stopped before Jed and jammed her hands into the pockets of her jacket. "What kept you? I've been waiting forever."

"The flight was late," Jed said. "And two hours is not forever."

"Well, it seemed like forever. You know how I hate to wait." The woman turned to Ysabel. "Who is she?"

"Ysabel Corbin," Jed answered. "Ysabel, this unmannerly person is Ronnie Dalton. Camerawoman *extraordinaire*. Unfortunately, she's significantly lacking in other areas."

"Corbin?" Ronnie's eyes flew to Jed's face. "Your wife?"

"My stepmother."

"Shades of Cinderella," Ronnie murmured as her gaze went over Ysabel. "They're not making them like they used to, are they?" A sudden gamin grin lit the angelic beauty of her face. "I should have know no one with any sense would have you, Jed."

"How do you do?" Ysabel said politely.

"Much better now that something interesting is afoot." Ronnie turned to Jed. "I rented a fifty-foot cruiser that has two cabins and stocked it with two weeks worth of supplies. When do we leave?"

"*You* stay here. *We* leave for San Miguel tonight."

Ronnie scowled mutinously. "The hell you say. I told you I—"

"I'm not after a story," Jed interrupted. "This trip is a purely personal indulgence and I'm not risking your neck."

"Family business?"

"You might call it that."

Ronnie glowered at Ysabel. "Is she going?"

Ysabel nodded. "It's necessary I go with Jed."

"For Lord's sake, Jed, she looks like she's made of whip cream," Ronnie exploded in disgust. "If you're not afraid of taking her, then I'm going too. I'll shoot some new footage and we'll kill two birds with one stone."

"I told you there's no story."

"Then we'll find one." Ronnie lifted her chin. "Maybe a follow-up on the one we did two years ago." With her thumb and forefinger she drew an imaginary caption in the air. "San Miguel Today."

"You went to San Miguel with Jed?" Ysabel asked.

"Of course, who do you think shot the film? He gets the glory, I do the work." Ronnie grimaced. "Hell, Jed would have shot everything upside down."

"I'm not that bad," Jed said testily.

"Yes, you are. Remember that gang war in the ghetto in Detroit?" Ronnie turned to go. "I'll run up to my room and get my bag. I'm all packed."

"No," Jed said firmly. "Read my lips, Ronnie. You aren't going."

"That's right. Use me and then throw me away," Ronnie said flippantly as she moved across the lobby toward the elevator. "It won't take me a minute. I'll be right back."

"Ronnie, dammit." Jed hurried after her. Looking at Ysabel over his shoulder, he tossed, "Wait here. Lord, she's stubborn. I'll be back as soon as I drum some sense into her."

Ysabel smothered a smile as he disappeared into the elevator with Ronnie. She settled on a nearby couch and made herself comfortable. It might be a long wait; Ronnie seemed to be a very determined woman. It was strange to see Jed at such a disadvantage; it certainly cast an entirely new light on his character. The relationship between them was clearly of long-standing, but Ysabel had caught no hint of a sexual undertone in the exchange she had witnessed. Jed clearly regarded Ronnie with the half tolerant, half exasperated affection Ysabel guessed he would a younger sister. The knowledge filled Ysabel with an odd relief.

Five minutes later the door of the elevator slid open and a scowling Ronnie Dalton stalked out and over to Ysabel. "Dammit, he's stubborn."

"That's what he said about you," Ysabel said mildly. "I take it he won?"

"For the moment." Ronnie smiled reluctantly. "I decided to retreat and prepare for a new foray."

"Where did he go?"

"I gave him my room key and he went up to make a few phone calls." Her frowned returned. "He told me to take care of you."

"Did he?" Ysabel smiled serenely as she rose to her feet. "That's not necessary, but you can take care of our luggage, if you like." She turned and moved toward the entrance. "Tell Jed I'll be back in a few hours."

"Wait!" Ronnie hurried after her out into the street. "You can't go anywhere. Jed told me to take care of you. He seems to think you'll fall apart if the wind disturbs one strand of hair."

"Hair . . . hmmm." Her gaze went to Ronnie's short curls. "I'll have to do something about that too." Turning to the doorman, she said, "Taxi, *por favor.*"

"Where are you going?" Ronnie asked.

"Shopping. I brought only three pairs of boots."

Ronnie's eyes widened. "And I thought I traveled light."

"They were the only useful things I had in my wardrobe." She limpidly gazed at Ronnie. "The rest was 'whip cream.'"

Ronnie looked slightly sheepish. "I was pretty rude, right?"

"Exceptionally."

"Sorry," she muttered. "I'm not good with people. Jed says I'm as belligerent as the devil."

She looked like a guilty little girl caught in some mischief, Ysabel thought. "And why are you belligerent?"

"It's my stupid face. No one takes me seriously," Ronnie said in disgust. "I look like one of those old ads for Ivory soap or an angel on a Christmas card. I have to show people I'm more than that."

"Jed said you're a fine camerawoman."

"You're darned tooting I am. The best."

Ysabel burst into laughter at the grimness of her tone. She found she genuinely liked her. Ronnie was refreshingly honest and blunt to the point of impudence, but beneath the bravado Ysabel caught nuances of vulnerability that touched her. "Would you like to come with me? I don't know anything about the shops in San Juan." She laughed joyously. "Correction, I don't know anything about shopping, period. It's a new experience for me."

Ronnie's skeptical gaze traveled over the elegance of Ysabel's dress. "Yeah, sure."

"No, really. I've always had my clothes made for me. Well, not on San Miguel but . . ." She shrugged. "I got them out of the welfare barrel at the mission there."

"Welfare? You?"

"My father was a missionary."

Ronnie's chin lifted defiantly. "And mine was a gunrunner."

She obviously expected the statement to shock Ysabel. "I see." Ysabel walked toward the taxi that had drawn up at the curb. "How interesting. I've never met a gunrunner. Was he good at his job?"

Ronnie blinked. "Not very."

"Well, are you coming?"

Ronnie hesitated and then hurried after her. "This town is into either tropical cruise wear or sophisticated chic. You won't find anything like that number you're wearing."

"Good. Will I be able to find what you're wearing?"

"Me?" Ronnie suddenly grinned. "Nope. I bought the jeans in a Goodwill store in Kansas City and won the jacket in a poker game in Tel Aviv."

"I don't know if they have Goodwill stores in San Juan and I've never learned how to play poker. Is there a place here I can find a reasonable facsimile?"

Ronnie thought for a moment and then turned to the doorman. "Send those bags sitting just inside the door up to room two thirteen." She opened the door of the cab. "Let's go."

"Where are we going?" Ysabel asked as she got into the taxi.

"To see if we can find a Banana Republic store in this burg."

Six

Jed was waiting in the lobby with a distinctly displeased expression when they walked in four hours later. "Where the hell have you been? Didn't it ever occur to you it would be courteous to—good God." His gaze wandered over Ysabel, starting from her white tennis shoes and moving to her fitted acid-washed jeans and crisp white chambray shirt. "You don't look like the same woman."

"I'm not the same woman." She put down the two shopping bags she carried. "That woman on Winter Island wasn't real. This is me. Ysabel."

He turned to Ronnie. "I suppose this is your doing?"

She shook her head. "I just went along for the ride, but I like the change. No more whip cream."

"I'm sorry if you don't approve," Ysabel said quietly.

"I didn't say I didn't like it. I haven't made up my mind. The metamorphosis just came as a shock."

His gaze went to the long thick single braid nestling against her breast. "At least you didn't cut your hair."

"I was tempted, but I didn't know how manageable my hair would be short. I decided it would be easier to care for in a braid." Ysabel turned to Ronnie. "May I use your room to pack all these things?"

"Sure," Ronnie said. "I won't be using it. I'm going down to the beach for a while."

"I thought you said beaches were boring," Jed said.

"Maybe I'm getting used to them." She met his gaze. "I don't suppose you've changed your mind about me going with you?"

"I have not."

"See you." She turned and started toward the door.

"We'll be leaving for the boat in about an hour. Will I see you before we leave?"

"Maybe," she answered over her shoulder.

"Ronnie, blast it, it's for the best."

"Sure."

"Wait a minute. You know—" He broke off as the glass door swung shut behind her. "What the devil is wrong with her?"

"Perhaps she's disappointed."

"Ronnie digs in and slugs it out, she doesn't sulk."

"She doesn't appear to be sulking to me." Ysabel's gaze followed Ronnie as she strolled down the street. "I like her very much." Her eyes shifted to Jed. "And I think you do too."

"If you can like a hair shirt." Jed picked up

Ysabel's two shopping bags. "I guess I'm used to the scamp."

She followed him into an elevator. "You've been together a long time?"

"Six years. We met in Nicaragua. She had just shot some footage of a rebel attack and came to my hotel to offer it to me in exchange for a job." He pushed the button, the doors slid closed and the cubicle started upward. "I said no. She was only an eighteen-year-old kid and some of the places my team goes aren't exactly safe."

That was an understatement, Ysabel thought with a shiver. But this time Jed would be safe in San Miguel. She would make sure nothing happened to him. "But you changed your mind?"

"She went out and managed to get to the front-lines and shot some dynamite footage. She also got herself shot in the arm while doing it. She came staggering into the hotel dining room, dripping blood, and put the tape on the table in front of me." He grimaced. "And promptly fainted dead away."

"And you gave her the job."

"No, not until she swore she'd follow me around the world and do the same thing until she had a story I couldn't refuse." He shrugged. "What could I do? It was better having her where I could keep an eye on her."

She chuckled. "Oh dear."

He frowned. "You seem to be enjoying this."

"I'm seeing another side of you. I never dreamed you could be this soft." The elevator door opened and she preceded him out into the hall. "Since I met you, I've always been the vulnerable one."

His lips tightened. "And I've always been cast as the cruel, heartless villain."

"I didn't say that. You were never cruel to me. I don't think you could be cruel."

"Don't be too sure."

His voice sounded oddly thick and she glanced at him over her shoulder. "I'm sure. You're hard and you can be ruthless, but you're fair and without malice. I know about—" She stopped as she saw his expression. "What's wrong?"

"Nothing." He tore his gaze from her lower body. "I've made up my mind about the jeans. I think I like the new Ysabel."

She felt heat flood her cheeks. "How . . . nice." He unlocked the door to her room and followed her inside. She nodded at the suitcase on the floor. "Will you put that on the bed for me? It won't take me long to pack and then we can get going."

He did as she asked. "There's no hurry."

She quickly reached into the shopping bag and pulled out two pairs of trousers and a blouse and bent over to place them in the suitcase. "You told Ronnie you wanted to be—" She inhaled sharply as she felt his hands cup her bottom from behind.

"We're not on any deadline. An hour or so won't matter," he said hoarsely. His hands moved up and down, squeezing, stroking. "This is the only thing I want right now, what I've been wanting since we left the cottage yesterday." His warm tongue darted in her ear. "And those tight jeans didn't help. I wanted to take you in that elevator. Take them off."

Her hands were trembling so much, she wasn't sure she could unfasten her jeans. In the exhilaration of leaving the island she had been only subliminally aware of the sexual magnetism pulling her toward Jed, but he'd merely had to touch her for it to come to the forefront. "They're not that tight. They just fit me well. It's not as if—" She broke off as he gently pinched her buttock. Her stomach clenched as she felt a liquid tingling in her womanhood. "You're sure we have time?"

"We'll make time." His hands slid around her belly to rub gently between her thighs. "How else am I going to get you out of my system if I—"

The phone shrilled on the table beside the bed.

"Damn!"

The phone rang again.

"I can't believe this," he muttered. "It's like an old movie cliché."

"Do we have to answer it?" she asked.

"Yes, blast it, it might be Ronnie. She manages to get in trouble at the drop of a hat. I can't risk not being accessible." His hands dropped away from her and he moved toward the telephone. "But she'd better have a damn good reason for calling." He picked up the receiver and bit out, "Corbin."

He listened a moment. "Can't he stay later?"

He listened again. "Okay, we'll be there."

He crashed down the receiver. "Finish packing. We have to get out of here."

"I thought you said—"

"I did. We'll have to wait until we're on the boat. That was James Garcia, the official I called at the State Department. He said if we can get to the embassy by five o'clock, he'll detain the clerk who can renew your passport. We'll stop there on the way to the harbor." He moved toward the door. "I'll

send up a bellboy for your suitcase in ten minutes."

"Where are you going?"

"I'll wait in the lobby. I have to get out of here."
He slanted her a searing glance over his shoulder.
"Or I'll say to hell with the damn passport and we'll
end up in bed. I can't take much more of this."

The door slammed behind him.

Four hours later they were over a hundred miles
out at sea, cutting through the waves in a forty-
foot cabin cruiser named *Lucky Venture*.

"It *is* going to be lucky," Ysabel said dreamily.

"What is?" Jed's hands tightly gripped the
wheel.

"The name of the boat's a good omen. I know it."

"I doubt if Ronnie was paying much attention to
omens when she leased the cruiser. She's one to
pay more attention to the practicalities of speed
and structure than to whimsies."

"I'm not so sure. She struck me as being a
strange mixture. . . ." She was suddenly aware
the engine had stopped. "Is something wrong?"

"No more than since we left the hotel." He
grasped her wrist and pulled her out of the wheel-
house and down the short flight of steps to the
cabin level. "I'm sorry to disturb your euphoric
mood, but I can't wait any longer."

She felt her breath leave her lungs and familiar
heat suffuse her body. It was going to happen.

"The only reason I waited until we were under-
way is that I didn't want to be interrupted again."
He threw open a door to reveal a teak-paneled

postage stamp-size cabin. Her gaze went immediately to the narrow bunk across the room.

Jed's gaze followed hers. "Not very wide but we won't need much room. Undress."

The order was succinct, made harsh by his need and a tension as erotic as an aphrodisiac.

Ysabel's hands flew to the buttons of her shirt.

"I see you're as obedient as usual," he said with a bittersweet smile. "And I thought you were a new woman."

"Why shouldn't I obey you? I made you a promise and besides I liked making love with you very much."

His hands clenched into fists. "It wasn't love," he said hoarsely.

She felt a stirring of pain but tried to smile. "I know but I couldn't think of what else to call it." She slipped out of her shirt and tossed it on the bed. "Why do you always make—"

"Achoo!"

The sneeze had not come from either of them but from somewhere across the cabin!

Ysabel's gaze flew to Jed, but he was already gliding silently toward a door across the cabin. He put a cautionary finger on his lips as he stood to the left of the door and reached for the knob.

"Oh rats! I've blown it, right?"

Ronnie's voice, Ysabel realized, relief surging through her.

Jed didn't share her reaction. He muttered a curse and threw open the door. "Get in here!"

Ronnie swaggered toward them but edged warily around Jed. "Isn't it weird how you always need to sneeze when it's least convenient? It must be something psychological that has to do with—"

"Explanation," Jed rapped.

"I wanted to come and I was bored out of my mind," Ronnie stated quickly. "And you might need me. Who's going to stay with the boat when you go ashore?"

"So you stowed away?"

"Well, I did decide it was better to not let you know I was on board until after you left San Juan. Actually, I thought we'd be a couple hundred miles out before you came down to go to bed." She made a face as her gaze met Ysabel's. "Sorry about the interruption. I really did think the trip was only business. You're not his usual type and he yells at you just like he does me."

"I don't yell at either one of you," Jed said frigidly.

"Well, you growl." Ronnie picked up Ysabel's shirt from the bunk and handed it to her. "You'd better put this on. It's getting cool in here."

"Thank you." Ysabel slipped on the shirt, fighting an absurd desire to giggle. "But I don't think it's the temperature."

"It was a fake sneeze, you know," Ronnie confided. "The wall between the cabins is so thin, I could practically hear you breathe, and I didn't know what else to do besides clearing my throat. I thought about dropping something but then Jed might have bolted in here and given me a karate chop before he realized I wasn't a threat. He's not exactly popular with the underworld element these days and gets a little edgy—"

"I almost did anyway," Jed interrupted grimly.

Ronnie ignored him as she told Ysabel earnestly, "I would have kept still if you'd only been doing it."

"Doing it?"

"Ronnie doesn't believe in euphemisms any more than I do," Jed said.

Ronnie nodded. "But you were talking, too, and eavesdropping is pretty low."

"Thank you," Ysabel said solemnly. "I appreciate the distinction."

"I guess we'll have to work out something." Ronnie's brow wrinkled in thought. "How about whenever you want to do it, you just tell me and I'll go for a walk on the deck?"

"I have a better idea," Jed said. "Why don't I just simplify matters and toss you overboard?"

She grinned. "I'd only swim after you. You're stuck with me."

He gazed at her for a moment and then turned on his heel and strode out of the cabin.

Ronnie flinched as the door slammed. "Maybe I'd better put on a life preserver." She glanced at Ysabel. "You mad at me too?"

"Surprised is more the word."

"Like I said, he didn't treat you like the others. He was all uptight and protective and didn't even glance at you and I thought . . ." she trailed off. "I promise I won't get in the way."

Her expression was suddenly so woebegone, Ysabel felt a surge of sympathy. "I know you won't. Once we get accustomed to the idea, I'm sure we'll both be very glad you're along."

"Really?" Ronnie brightened. "You're not just being polite to me?"

"I believe this situation goes slightly beyond the bounds of courtesy."

Ronnie's wistful gaze went to the doorway through which Jed had disappeared. "He's really mad at me this time. Maybe I'd better go up and try to cool him down."

"Let me do it." Ysabel turned and moved toward the door. "I think you'd better stay out of sight for a while."

"Oh." Ronnie thought for a minute. "I know, I'll go fix supper."

"Are you a good cook?"

"Rotten," she admitted cheerfully. "But I figure anyone can make an omelet and Jed knows me well enough to recognize it as a peace gesture."

But indigestion might not improve his temper. Ysabel resisted the impulse to vocalize the thought as she hurried up the steps to the deck.

She saw Jed standing at the rail, looking out over the sea, the line of his spine rigid, his demeanor forbidding.

"She really is upset that you're angry with her," Ysabel said quietly as she joined him at the rail.

"That won't stop her from doing the same thing again if it suits her," Jed said curtly. "And it won't help the present situation one iota."

"She seems to be willing to make any adjustments to—"

"A great choice. I'm supposed to either announce my intentions to 'do it' to all and sundry or subject you to a silent witness in the next cabin."

"I made no objection."

"Well, I do." He turned on her, his eyes blazing. "I know you'll take anything I hand out to you, but it's shoddy and I won't have you put— Why the devil are you grinning at me?"

"Because you're funny." And because happiness had surged through her in a golden tide at his words. "I believe beneath that tough exterior lies a Galahad."

"Bull."

"Then why are you trying to guard my delicate sensibilities?"

He scowled at her. "How the hell do I know? It's just not— I'll get over it."

She shook her head. "I don't think you will and I believe you know it and that's why you're so angry."

He wearily rubbed the back of his neck. "I've been angry since the moment I met you."

"Since you met the Winter Bride," she corrected. "But I'm not that woman and I never was. How can I convince you?"

"It seems we're going to have a long time to explore the subject," he said dryly. "It may be the longest four days of my life."

"But perhaps this has happened for the best," she said eagerly. "We can get to know each other and you can see I'm not—"

"For Lord's sake, don't you understand? That's the whole point. I don't *want* to get to know you." The words exploded with barely contained violence. "As long as you're just a woman in my bed I'll be able to—"

"I'm sorry," she rushed in, trying to stop him and the fierce pain from igniting within her. "If that's what you want, perhaps you should reconsider Ronnie's suggestion to—"

"Stop saying you're sorry!" His hands tightened on the rail. "Why should you be sorry? None of this is your fault."

She smiled shakily. "It's hard to break a habit. I was always the one to blame if something went wrong."

"Blast it, are you crying?"

"No, of course not."

"Then you're damn close." He turned her around to face him and looked down into her shimmering eyes. "Some Galahad." He reached out and gently caressed her cheek. A multitude of emotions flickered over his face before he sighed. "Okay."

Tenderness again, coming as unexpectedly as it had those two occasions in the cottage. She knew he was struggling against it, but she didn't care how it had sprung into being. For this moment, it was here. She stood very still beneath his touch, wanting it to go on forever. "Okay, what?"

"Anything you want. Just don't cry." His voice was gruff. "All right, until we get to San Miguel I get to know the new woman and you put up with a man who is definitely no gentle knight." He scowled. "But only until we reached San Miguel and get rid of Ronnie. Deal?"

She smiled brilliantly. "Oh yes, deal." She started to turn away and then thought of something. "Where . . . do I sleep?"

"With me. That hasn't changed. I have no intention of letting you become accustomed to sleeping anywhere else. Any objection?"

"No, I just thought . . . I could sleep up here on deck."

"No way." He turned his back on her and looked out over the ocean. "We sleep together."

Jed didn't come to the cabin until nearly midnight, but she was still awake. She went rigid in the bed, but he didn't speak and a moment later she heard the sounds of his undressing in the darkness. She tried to look away but found she couldn't. She could see only a moving shadow, but that made no difference. The memory of his nudity in the cabin was suddenly before her. The powerful line of his thighs, the tight buttocks, the jutting arousal of— Heat suffused her and she quickly blocked the image.

His skin gleamed pale in the darkness as he came toward the bunk, but it wasn't pale, she remembered. He was tan and the dark hair of his chest was peppered with the same silver as his hair. He stopped beside the bunk and she could hear the rhythmic sound of his breathing as he stood over her. "I hoped you'd be asleep."

"How did you know I wasn't?" she whispered.

"I could sense you watching me. It was disconcerting as hell."

"I'm sorry. I couldn't sleep."

"Scoot over."

She quickly moved over to the opposite side of the bed. "It's late. I thought you'd changed your mind."

"And that I'd bunk on deck?" He slipped into bed beside her. "Why? I gave you my reasons and, besides, I like my comfort." He laughed harshly.

"Though this bunk may prove a bed of nails before this trip is over."

He lay there for a few moments, unmoving, every muscle locked and tense. "For Lord's sake, go to sleep. I can *feel* you there."

"I'm having a little difficulty adjusting to sleeping with a man."

He chuckled mirthlessly. "You have no problem with letting me make love to you, but sleeping with me is too personal?"

"It's different. Sleeping requires a lack of tension."

"And a lowering of your guard." He added bitterly, "And you can't do that with—"

The door to the next cabin slammed and they heard Ronnie whistling cheerfully . . . and loudly.

Jed cursed beneath his breath. "I believe we're being reminded we're not alone."

"This doesn't seem to be working." She moistened her lips. "You're getting angry again."

"I'm *hurting*, dammit."

"You are?" Then there was no question he would continue with abstinence. She tried to smother her disappointment as she thought for a moment. "Couldn't we do it quietly?"

She sensed him grow rigid and then felt the mattress shift as he turned to look at her. "What?"

"I'd be perfectly willing to do anything you ask that would help you. You'd have to tell me what to do, of course."

"Of course," he said hoarsely.

"I remember crying out before, but perhaps you could put your hand over my mouth when you—"

"*Shut up.*"

The violence of his tone surprised her. "I was only trying to help."

"Help? You're killing me." He suddenly drew her into his arms and she immediately stiffened as she encountered warm, hard flesh. "Stop tensing. I'm not going to take you up on your offer. I just had to *touch* you." His hand moved exploringly over her. "What are you wearing?"

"A sleepshirt from Banana Republic."

His hand cupped her breast, weighing it in his palm. The heat was growing and an ache of emptiness was starting between her thighs. Yet, even as her breasts swelled in response, she felt a sinking feeling in the pit of her stomach.

"Does the shirt bother you?" she asked. "It's really only an oversized T-shirt, but I could take it off."

"Don't say— No, keep it on."

The shower suddenly started in the next cabin and Ronnie began to sing.

"She can't hear us now," Ysabel said quietly.

"I know that." His tone was distinctly edgy. "You appear very accommodating."

"A promise is a promise."

He went still as he caught the inflection in her tone. "But you're disappointed."

She hadn't realized she had revealed the disappointment that was part of the turmoil she was experiencing. "I don't have the right to be disappointed. You're in discomfort and we agreed you'd call the shots. I knew lovemaking was a possibility."

"And, of course, since I'm in need, it's your duty to supply what I need." He drew a deep breath and then his hand left her breast. "I'm afraid you've been trained a little too well."

She wanted him to put his hand back.

Instead, he pressed her head into the hollow of his shoulder. "Yes, a promise is a promise. I guess I was in danger of forgetting I made one too."

"It's all right, we can—"

"Hush. Lie still," he said thickly. "Lie very, very still."

Minutes passed as she lay there, excruciatingly conscious of his warmth, the soft abrasion of the hair of his chest against her cheek, the scent of soap and spice cologne. Gradually she found herself relaxing, accepting the intimacy. "It's . . . not so bad, is it?"

Jed didn't answer.

Another moment passed before she changed position, shifted a little closer.

"Don't do that!"

As she started to scoot away, he stopped her, holding her captive. "Sorry," he said gruffly. "Let's take this one step at a time." His hand began to stroke her hair, quieting her. "Just go to sleep."

How could she go to sleep when she felt as if she were lying next to a live grenade ready to explode?

"Let go, Ysabel . . ."

She loved the way he said her name, lingering like a dark sonata on the syllables, and the stroking of his hand on her hair had its own deep rhythm.

Once again she relaxed against him. "If you change your mind, tell me."

"I wish you'd stop offering. I'm absolutely not

going to change my mind." He added in a barely audible tone, "Maybe."

"Well, if you do . . ." She yawned. She was beginning to feel drowsy, she realized in surprise. Odd, when only a few moments before she had been a galaxy away from sleep. Only a little drowsy, she assured herself. She was sure it would be hours before she was relaxed enough to go to sleep. . . .

Seven

"What are you writing?" Ysabel asked.

Jed looked up with a grin from the computer he was cradling on his crossed knees. "I was wondering how long it was going to take you to display a modicum of curiosity. You've sat there watching me for the past three days and haven't said a word."

"We've talked," she protested. For a moment she lost track of what they had been saying as she looked at him. The sun shimmered on his silver hair, and his eyes were bluer than the sea around them. She tore her gaze away from his face and shifted to his hands. Strong, tanned hands, deft on the computer keys, more deft on . . . She said quickly, "I thought you'd tell me if you wanted me to know."

"That politeness again."

"I can't help it if I was well brought up. My foster father believed civility was close to godliness."

"Your foster father?"

Darn it, it had been a mistake to have mentioned John. She should have known it would immediately arouse Jed's curiosity.

When she didn't reply, he went on, "Ronnie mentioned you'd told her your father was a missionary. He was really your foster father?"

"Yes."

"As communicative as always, I see." To her relief he didn't pursue the subject. "Courtesy is an anachronism in this day and age but then so are you." He raised a mocking brow. "What prompted you to commit such a heinous crime as asking me such a personal question as what I'm writing?"

She smiled uncertainly. "You're making fun of me."

"Am I?"

She tucked back a strand of hair the wind had blown over her cheek. "Yes, but I don't think you mean it unkindly." She looked out at the sea. "You're teasing me, aren't you?"

"Perhaps a little. It's easy to do. You're such a serious little animal." He went back to the original question. "Why now?"

"I don't know. I suppose I feel . . . closer to you now. You've been very kind to me since we left San Juan."

"You mean I've been civilized."

A sudden smile lit her face "I didn't say that."

"You didn't have to say it." He continued to stare at her face with narrowed eyes and for a moment she didn't think he was going to answer her. Then he said, "I'm writing a book. Didn't you know every newsman thinks he has a best-seller in him?"

"Is it about your experiences in the field?"

"No. Fiction."

"What kind of fiction?"

"Good heavens, two questions in a row. That must be traumatic for you. Historical."

Her expression must have reflected her surprise because he chuckled. "You don't think it's my métier?"

"I've never met anyone who was more contemporary minded."

"We all need a certain amount of escape in this high-tech world."

"And you make your escape by going back in history?"

"I'm not saying the people then didn't have their own problems, some of them insurmountable, but life was simpler and less complicated."

"Yet you've chosen a career in which you're continually confronted with the most complicated problems of the world."

"I didn't say I couldn't deal with modern life. I just need a rest now and then." He raised his brows. "Is your curiosity satisfied now?"

"Yes, thank you." It wasn't true. She had found her curiosity about him growing by leaps and bounds in their enforced intimacy. She had not known what to expect, but she hadn't been prepared for the Jed Corbin of the last two days. He had practically ignored her while he was working, but, after he had finished, he had made coffee and talked to her casually about his experiences, asked her about her studies and opinions. During the day he treated her as platonically as he did Ronnie, and at night he had held her with almost fraternal gentleness. At no time had she been conscious of the anger and resentment he had previously exhibited.

"Another thank you?" He grimaced. "I thought we'd moved away from that."

"I'll work on it. It's difficult to break habits ingrained in childhood." She leaned back against the rail and tilted her head. "Why have you changed toward me?"

"You think I've changed?" He shook his head. "Not really. I've just tried to keep my promise."

"And promises are important to you?"

He nodded. "I've watched diplomats and heads of state make promises that affect entire populations and then not follow through for the sake of convenience or ambition." He gazed past her, his eyes fixed unseeingly on the sea. "Perhaps that's one of the reasons I like history. In this world we all need a code of honor like the ones back in King Arthur's day."

"From what I understand those knights broke that code rather frequently."

"But a black-and-white code existed and when it was broken, you knew it was broken. The lines were cleaner and better defined. You didn't slip into quicksand because you didn't know it was there."

She chuckled. "Perhaps I wasn't far wrong when I called you Galahad. You definitely have a medieval turn of mind."

He smiled faintly. "Not Galahad. Lancelot maybe. He was much more apt to break the rules and grab something for himself."

"Guinevere?"

He nodded. "And glory and a piece of the pie. He was more of a materialist than Galahad."

"You seem very well versed in Camelot."

"Growing up with the Winter Bride bred a certain curiosity. She captured my imagination and I wanted to know who she was, where she came from. . . ." He paused and his gaze shifted back to Ysabel's face. "And why she looked so frightened."

"She wasn't frightened, only unsure and a little nervous. She knew she could handle whatever was waiting for her. I've always thought her husband in that castle on the hill would have a woman to reckon with."

His expression hardened. "Well, I suppose you should know."

The moment of warmth and confidence had vanished and she felt a flicker of regret. She forced a smile. "Yes, I had plenty of time to study and think about her over the years." She swiftly looked away from him to Ronnie, who was standing at the wheel at the far end of the boat. "She's been steering for three hours. Perhaps I should go relieve her."

His expression softened as his glance followed hers. "Heaven forbid. If that firecracker doesn't have something to do, she'll get out her camera and we'll be in real trouble. She'll probably decide to don scuba gear and try to film those dolphins that have been following us."

"True." Ysabel had discovered Ronnie's crackling energy could be exhausting as well as exhilarating. The girl seemed to have to be busy every second or she became restless. She had taken over the cooking, the cleaning, and lately had commandeered the running of the cruiser. "Who did you think might be in that cabin?"

"What?"

"Ronnie said you were always edgy these days."

He shrugged. "You don't specialize in investigative reporting and not have enemies. I've had a few death threats."

She gazed at him, stunned. "Death threats."

"Why are you surprised? You knew about Marino."

"But I thought he was the only one and he's on San Miguel. Why are you just walking around unprotected? Why don't you have bodyguards?"

"They'd get in my way."

She felt like hitting him. "Life is precious, dammit, and you go around risking . . ." She trailed off, unable to continue.

"You're angry." A slow smile lit his face. "I've never really seen you angry before. It's . . . interesting."

"I'm not angry. Why should I be angry at someone who could be so abysmally dumb as to wander around as if he owned the earth when people are trying to kill him?" She jumped to her feet. "And stop grinning at me!" She stalked across the deck to the opposite side. Her hands were trembling as they reached out to grasp the rail. Anger, she assured herself, it was anger, not fear for him that had struck her to the heart.

He followed her, but she refused to look at him. "Go away."

"Why? I'm finding your reaction fascinating. You know how curious I am."

"I won't be dissected."

"Isn't it my turn? You've probed me enough this afternoon and I still haven't found out any more about you than you like pizza and hate artichokes." His voice was soft, velvet persuasion.

"Talk to me, Ysabel. How can I become acquainted with this new woman if you won't trust me enough to let me in and get to know her."

Dear Heaven, she wanted to talk to him, to let the words flow into him so she would no longer be alone. She opened her mouth to speak and then closed it. A moment later she said shakily, "Later. When we reach San Miguel."

She could sense his sudden stiffening. His tone took on a sharp edge. "I'm getting very tired of that line. What difference does it make whether you tell me now or a day from now?"

She didn't answer.

"No? Well, that puts me in my place, doesn't it?" He turned on his heel and strode away from her.

She drew a deep breath and closed her eyes. She had hurt him. Her reaction to the thought of Jed in danger had startled her and it was as if something inside her had exploded. She had never thought she was capable of hurting Jed, but she knew pain too well herself not to recognize it when she heard it. She knew she wasn't being fair, but fear and caution were too engraved in her mind and spirit to permit her to be open with him.

Jed was tough. He would get over it. They would reach San Miguel tomorrow and once there she would be able to be honest with him.

Yes, everything would be all right once they reached San Miguel.

Jed was grimly silent the rest of the afternoon and by the end of the evening meal even Ronnie was gazing at him with puzzlement and trepidation.

When he had finished eating, he strode out of the galley without a word.

"Whew!" Ronnie made a face as she stood up and began to stack the dishes. "What the heck did you do to him?"

"Nothing."

"Don't tell me that. I know him."

"He . . . thinks I don't trust him."

"Then tell him he's wrong."

Ysabel didn't answer as she carried her own plate to the sink.

"You *don't* trust him." Ronnie gazed at her in disbelief. "Are you nuts? Jed's like the Rock of Gibraltar. I thought you were savvy enough to realize that bad-boy persona was all publicity hype."

Ysabel didn't look at her as she unplugged the coffee maker. "I'm glad you've found him trustworthy."

"Trustworthy? He's saved my neck more than once," Ronnie said. "He may growl and snap when things don't go right, but he's always there when the going gets rough and he stays until the shooting stops."

"And what then?"

"What else do you want me to say?" Ronnie shook her head in bewilderment. "Isn't that enough?"

Enough for Ronnie, who was as wary in her own way as Jed, but it wouldn't be enough for Ysabel. "I'd rather not talk—"

"What the devil do I care what you want?" Ronnie's eyes were suddenly blazing. "You hurt him. Now go do something about it."

Ysabel's eyes widened. "And what do you suggest I do?"

"How do I know? You did the damage. Repair it."

She felt as if she had been attacked by a bull-terrier. "You make it sound so simple."

"It is simple. You screw up, you fix it."

She gazed at Ronnie curiously. "And what would you do if I didn't fix it?"

"Don't ask." Ronnie turned on the water. "I like you, but Jed and I go back a long way."

There was no missing the implied threat in Ronnie's words, and Ysabel's smile slowly faded. The girl's fierce loyalty to Jed was as passionate as all her other emotions, and Ysabel wondered wistfully what experiences had cemented that loyalty.

"Go on." Ronnie began briskly scrubbing the dishes. "I'll be busy here for a while and then I'm going to take my camera out on deck and work."

"In the dark?"

Ronnie ignored the question. "I'll probably be working all night." She paused meaningfully. "You understand?"

"Perfectly."

"You make it all right with him any way you have to."

"Are you suggesting I sleep with him to soothe his feelings?"

"Why not? Sex isn't important and it seems to make men feel better." She frowned. "And this time my being around made Jed feel awkward. It's pretty weird since he's never been shy about sex

A Magical World of Enchantment Awaits You When You're Loveswept!

Your heart will be swept away with Loveswept Romances when you meet exciting heroes you'll fall in love with...beautiful heroines you'll identify with. Share the laughter, tears and the passion of unforgettable couples as love works its magic spell. These romances will lift you into the exciting world of love, charm and enchantment!

You'll enjoy award-winning authors such as Iris Johansen, Sandra Brown, Kay Hooper and others who top the best-seller lists. Each offers a kaleidoscope of adventure and passion that will enthrall, excite and exhilarate you with the magic of being Loveswept!

- ♥ **We'd like to send you 6 new novels to enjoy—_risk free_!**
- ♥ **There's no obligation to buy.**
- ♥ **6 exciting romances—plus your _free gift_—brought right to your door!**
- ♥ **Convenient money-saving, time-saving home delivery!**

Join the Loveswept at-home reader service and we'll send you 6 new romances about once a month— before they appear in the bookstore! You always get 15 days to preview them before you decide. Keep only those you want. Each book is yours for only $2.25* That's a total savings of $3.00 off the retail price for each 6 book shipment.

ENJOY. . .

♥ 6 Romance Novels–Risk Free! ♥ Exclusive Novel Free!
♥ Money Saving Home Delivery!

before. I remember in Mexico we shared a house with a prostitute and they went at it like—"

"I don't believe Jed would want you to discuss this with me," Ysabel said quickly.

"Maybe not." She shook her head. "Like I said, he's weird about you."

"Weirder than you know," Ysabel muttered as she headed for the door.

"You'll fix it?" Ronnie demanded.

"Will you please stop nagging me about—" She stopped as she realized there was genuine concern as well as belligerence in Ronnie's expression. Perhaps she should have been annoyed with her, but she suddenly realized why she had been willing to let Ronnie bulldoze her. Since the moment she had hurt Jed, she had been miserable about it and desperately wanted to make things right between them. She smiled gently. "Ronnie, don't worry. I'll fix it."

He stood at the rail, his legs astride, staring out into the darkness, appearing about as approachable as an iceberg.

She hesitated and then crossed the deck to stand beside him. "I know you don't like me to say I'm sorry but, if I don't, Ronnie may throw me overboard."

He didn't answer.

"At least growl at me so I'll know I'm not completely beyond the pale."

"I don't growl. Animals growl."

"I'd say you do a fairly good imitation." She put her hand on his arm and felt the muscles harden beneath her touch. "Ronnie says I have to make things right with you."

"Charming. I'm not sure whether this apology is coming from you or Ronnie."

"It's coming from me. What can I do to show you how sorry I am?"

"What did Ronnie suggest?" he asked caustically.

She smiled. "Sex."

He made a low exclamation and turned to face her, his blue eyes glittering silver in the moonlight. "I don't find that amusing."

"I did. She seems to think sex is like an aspirin or a Band-Aid."

"I could have used that particular Band-Aid in the last few days. Lying in that bunk beside you, I felt as if I were bleeding to death."

Her smile disappeared. "Really? I would never have guessed it."

"Because I made you a promise." He added through his teeth, "Take your hand away."

She spoke quickly, not looking at him. "You should have told me. I thought you were over it. It's all right, you know. We made an agreement. If you want—"

"To jump your bones?" he finished harshly. He took her hand off his arm and put it on the rail. "No, thank you. It's not enough anymore."

She inhaled sharply, trying to smother a leap of hope at his words. "It's not?"

"You know it's not. I *told* you I didn't want to get to know you. I knew it would get in the way."

Hope died almost at the instance of birth. "You

mean it gets in the way of your conception of the Winter Bride," she said dully.

"Stop putting words in my mouth."

"That must be what you mean."

"I don't know what I meant. I haven't been able to think straight since I met you." He glared down at her. "And it's not going to get any better if I let you lull me off to carnal bliss every time I run into one of these walls you throw up against me."

"What do you want? What would make it better?"

"Answers."

"I can't talk about San Miguel," she whispered. "I don't have the right."

"Half a loaf is better than zilch. Talk about Winter Island."

"I'd rather not, if you don't mind," she said stiltedly.

"I do mind."

"Why? It's all in the past now."

"Because I need to know you."

"I told you I'm not that woman on the island."

"The hell you aren't. You couldn't have lived those years in a vacuum."

"You think not? I did live—" She broke off as she realized she was being unfair again. Because she desperately wanted to block out that period, she was closing Jed out entirely. "What do you want to know?"

"Everything. What you felt, what you did, what you thought."

"I think you're still trying to decipher the Winter Bride," she said with a bittersweet smile. "You knew your father very well so you must know what my life was like."

"I don't know and it's like a hot brand inside me, thinking about you and him and wondering . . ." His tone was unrelenting. "Tell me."

"It was difficult." She crossed her arms over her chest to still their trembling. "I had to learn . . . You must understand my nature isn't gentle. At sixteen I was a young hellion. But Arnold perceived the Bride to be gentle, so I had to become the Bride. I had to learn to walk, to move, to speak only when spoken to, to obey his every wish without question."

"And Betty's wish?"

"Yes, she was Arnold's second in command. To disobey her was to disobey Arnold and would reap the same punishment."

"Physical abuse."

"On Arnold's part. Betty soon found her own way to punish me and keep me submissive." Her nails dug into her upper arms. "I think I preferred being struck. She flayed my spirit."

"Good God, why did you stay?" he said thickly.

"It was necessary. You can do anything you have to do if it's necessary." Her eyes were stinging and she blinked rapidly to keep back the tears. "Have I said enough? I'd like to forget it now, please."

"Lord." He suddenly turned and swept her into his arms and rocked her back and forth in an agony of sympathy. "What am I going to do with you?"

Keep holding me, she wanted to tell him. She felt treasured, cosseted as she hadn't since she was a small child. "Is it enough?"

"Not by a long shot," he said huskily as his hand cupped the back of her head. "How the hell did you survive it?"

It was easier to talk now, almost as if he were absorbing the pain of those years. "By living in a vacuum, studying, by trying to win something from every defeat." She nestled closer, speaking dreamily. "That's the important thing—not to ever let yourself be totally defeated. Every time I was forced into a situation where I had to yield, I tried to find a way to win something for myself. From subjugation you can learn patience, from ugliness you can learn beauty, from cruelty you can learn—"

"Wait." She felt him stiffen against her and he slowly pushed her away, to look down into her eyes. "And what did you win from me?"

She moistened her lips. "What do you mean?"

"When you came to my bed that day at the cottage you said you had your own reasons for doing it. What were they? How were you going to survive that particular defeat?"

"What difference does it make?"

"I want to know, dammit."

He wasn't going to be deterred and she would not lie to him. "A child."

His eyes widened. "What?"

"I love children. I would like one of my own." She spoke quickly, her gaze fastened on the top button of his shirt. "Don't you see, it was the only way I could win. You'd placed me in a position of subjugation."

"I must have misinterpreted your response," he said caustically. "I thought we both won in that encounter."

"Pleasure? Of course, there was pleasure but you still forced that pleasure on me. I didn't come seeking. I came at your command because it was something I had to do." She met his gaze. "Can't you understand? I had to win something for myself."

"My child?" His hands tightened on her shoulders. "You're not on the Pill?"

"No." She added, "I may not have become pregnant, of course, but I hope very much that I did. That day may have been my only chance for a child because, even if I found another man I could respond to, I don't believe I could tolerate a so-called relationship." She shuddered. "I never want to be caught in that cage again."

"So you play hit-and-run and walk away with my child."

"Perhaps." She straightened her shoulders. "But you needn't worry about it. It has nothing to do with you."

"The hell it doesn't. I'm not a walking sperm bank. I have feelings, dammit." His lips tightened. "And I learned through bad example how not to be a father. One of the rules is that you don't walk away from responsibility."

"You're not being reasonable."

"How would you know what reason is? Your life has been nothing but compromises."

How could she deny the truth? "I didn't mean to upset you again." She tried to smile. "Ronnie's going to be—"

"Oh yes, we're back to Ronnie's philosophy. 'Soothe the hurt with good old-fashioned sex.'" His lips twisted sardonically. "But she doesn't know what might result from that application, does she?" He released her and turned away. "Well, I'm through 'commanding' you to my bed and I'm through being used so you can win your own little battles."

"You don't understand."

"I do understand." The glance he shot her over his shoulder held an element of torment as well as frustration. "That's the trouble. Half of me wants to pick you up and cuddle you and tell you it's all right that you felt you had to use me, and the other half wants to strangle you." He strode toward the steps. "Go to bed."

"Where are you going?"

"To the galley to see Ronnie. I feel in the mood for a cutthroat game of cards and she's a hell of a lot better at poker than she is at giving advice."

"It looks deserted." Ysabel's gaze searched the vacant streets and ramshackle huts of the small village hugging the coastline. "Where are all the people?"

"Dead," Jed said. "Four of Juan Perez's rebel band were wounded in a raid and came here to take refuge. When Marino discovered they were here, he decided to make an example of the village. He ordered every man, woman, and child killed and the village abandoned."

"Charming man," Ronnie said ironically as she guided the cruiser closer to the pier.

Ysabel's hands tightened on the rail. "He's a monster."

Ronnie gave Jed a sidelong glance from beneath

her lashes. "I vote we get some footage that will kick Congress into giving more aid to the rebels. How about it?"

"The CIA has been trying to find a way to snag Marino for the last year, but it's not likely that Congress will give any overt help after Nicaragua."

"We can try."

"Perez's rebels have been doing pretty well on their own lately."

"A couple of choice pictures wouldn't hurt. Is Ramon going to meet us here at the village?" Ronnie cut off the engine and pressed the button that lowered the anchor.

"Us?" Jed asked dryly. "I thought you were going to stay on board and guard the cruiser."

"I decided the cruiser would be safe here and you might need me more to help with this mysterious search." Ronnie grinned impudently at him. "Besides, Ramon always liked me best."

"Which doesn't say much. He doesn't really like anyone or anything but his printing press."

"Who is this Ramon?" Ysabel asked.

"Ramon Damirez. He publishes an underground newspaper in the capital and has contacts with the rebels. Marino wants his neck as much as he does mine."

"Well, is he going to meet us?" Ronnie asked.

Jed nodded as he jumped down to the pier and then helped Ysabel. "At the priest's living quarters at the chapel where he met us when we came here two years ago." He released Ysabel at once and turned to help Ronnie, but she had already jumped to the pier. "I had to call in a few favors to get him here, but I don't promise that he'll be very eager to help. He has more important fish to fry than searching for lost objects."

"I believe he'll be willing to help me find this one." She felt strange to be back in San Miguel after all these years. This was the island of her birth yet now it felt as alien as Winter Island. She moved quickly down the pier. "Are you sure the village is entirely deserted?"

"According to Ramon."

"Still we'd better be cautious. Marino has spies everywhere."

"You seem very aware of the situation here."

"Not enough. If I'd known more, I wouldn't have needed your help. You trust this Ramon?"

"Implicitly," Jed said. "But then I evidently have more faith in human nature than you do."

Ysabel felt a wrenching pain at the barb but carefully schooled her expression not to reveal it. "Perhaps you can afford faith." She quickened her pace. "At any rate, in this case I'll have to rely on your judgment." She caught sight of the small white stucco chapel at the edge of the deserted village, and a leap of hope went through her. Alien land or not, she was here. Impulsively she turned to Jed and whispered, "Thank you. You don't know what this means to me."

"You're right about that." As he saw the luminous eagerness begin to fade from her face, his expression softened. "I haven't done anything yet," he said gruffly. "We'll have to see what Ramon has to say."

Eight

"*Madre de Dios!* You brought me here for this?"
Ramon's dark eyes were dagger-hard in his plump
face as he glared at Ysabel. "I'm not in the business
of reclaiming family treasures, Jed."

"Don't get on your high horse, Ramon." Ronnie
grinned at him as she hoisted herself to sit on a
table. "She needs your help and you know what a
courtly gentleman you are beneath all those prick-
les."

Ramon turned his glower on her. "I'm a patriot,
not a gentleman. The two do not mix in this
country."

"So much for him liking you better," Jed murmured. "I need this favor, Ramon."

"Perhaps I'd better explain just what it is *I* need."
Ysabel took a step forward to face Ramon. "It's
possible he won't have the courage to help me."

Ramon's tone dipped another ten degrees. "I
don't have to prove my courage to you, Señora."

She took a deep breath. "You call yourself a patriot, but are you brave enough to tweak Marino's nose and steal his most valuable possession?" She heard Ronnie's swift intake of breath and sensed Jed's sudden stillness but ignored them both, her gaze focused on Ramon. "Are you a patriot enough for that, Señor Damirez?"

Ramon's expression was suddenly wary. "And what is that possession?"

"His son."

Jed muttered an expletive. "What the devil are you talking about? Marino has no son."

Ysabel had caught a flicker of expression on Ramon's face. "I believe Señor Damirez knows better," she said softly. "Don't you, señor?"

"Ramon?" Jed asked.

"There are certain . . . rumors."

"What rumors?"

"Of a boy being held at the *Castillo del Fuego* whom the General visits every month." Ramon's voice was cautious as he gazed at Ysabel. "How did you know of the boy?"

Ysabel hesitated and then said in a rush, "I'm his sister."

"Holy Toledo." Ronnie closed her mouth, which had dropped open, and began to chuckle. "And Jed said there was no story here."

"The lady failed to confide in me," Jed said coldly.

Ysabel gazed at him pleadingly. "Can't you see I couldn't tell you about Steven? What if you'd thought the danger was too great and not agreed to bring me? I've waited seven years to free him from that *castillo*."

"They call him Manuel now," Ramon said. "You're truly Marino's daughter?"

Her lips twisted bitterly. "I was born of his seed, but I am *not* that monster's daughter."

"You can't have it both ways."

"I can and I will." Her hands clenched into fists at her sides. "I'm not here to discuss my parentage. I have a plan for his escape, but I need help to get him from the *castillo* back to the cruiser."

"What plan?" Ramon asked.

"My late husband has had a guard at the *castillo* in his pay for the last seven years. After his death I took over the contact. The guard's name is Pedro Ridelez. When I give him the word, he'll tell Steven to be in the courtyard at eight in the morning the day after tomorrow, open the gate, and delay the guard manning the gate for twenty minutes. That's all the time we'll need."

"And you intend to just walk out of there with him?"

"The *castillo* isn't a high-security installation, and Steven hasn't tried to escape for the past three years. We'll have the element of surprise."

"And what if he doesn't want to escape? From what we can learn the boy's not treated badly. He's had tutors and good food and fine clothes. We weren't even sure if he was a prisoner. No one can question Marino's charisma when he wishes to exert it."

"Don't worry, he wants to escape."

"How do you know, if you haven't seen him for seven years?"

"My last letter from him was only six months ago." She smiled without mirth. "And I'm sure he hasn't changed his mind about Marino. Marino shot my mother and foster father, John Belfort, to death before our eyes. It's not a sight a boy would easily forget."

"Or a girl," Jed murmured.

"We're not talking about me," Ysabel said impatiently. "Señor Damirez, there's a glade in the jungle a mile and a half from the *castillo*. All I ask is that Perez finds a way to get word to Ridelez and has a helicopter in the glade ready to take off at eight fifteen."

"All? There will be great danger," Ramon said slowly.

Ysabel could tell he was tempted and pushed the advantage. "Yes, but look at the story you'd have for your newspaper, and Marino would be wiping egg off his face for a year."

"True." A sudden smile lit Ramon's face. "A sight I'd love to see."

"Then do it—free him." Her voice vibrated with intensity. "Help me."

"It's too pat, too easy. You can't be sure the situation at the *castillo* is the same as Ridelez described to you."

"Ridelez sent me a map of the terrain and told me there's a deserted shack where he used to live about five miles from the *castillo*. I need you to take me there. I can stay there while I look over the security and make sure it's safe to make a move. I'll need you to take me to the shack early tomorrow morning."

"So now it's not only Perez but I who am to become involved?"

"I'm asking you only to drive a car, not fight for me."

"Even driving you may be a risk if we're stopped by the *guardia*. The *castillo* is over a hundred miles from here." Ramon hesitated. "We'll see. I'll contact Perez at his base in the hills and we'll discuss it."

"When will I know?"

He shrugged. "If we decide to help, I'll be here tomorrow at dawn to take you to Ridelez's shack. If I'm not here, I'd advise you to go back to your cruiser and leave San Miguel."

She shook her head. "If you're not here, I'll get Steven out myself. I'm not leaving San Miguel without him."

Grudging respect flickered over Ramon's face. "Bold words. I almost believe you could do it." He turned to Jed. "And what about you?"

"I made her a promise," Jed said. "I'll keep it."

"It may be a very expensive promise." Ramon nodded at the arched doorway across the room. "I took the precaution of bringing a few items of food for you. They're on the counter in the kitchen." His expression changed from sourness to sadness as his gaze traveled around the room, which had been stripped of every piece of furniture but a rickety table jammed against the wall. His glance lingered on the white outline of a cross on the wall where the priest's precious crucifix must have been displayed. "Lord knows there's nothing left in this village." He strode toward the back door. "Perhaps I'll see you in the morning."

"Wait," Ysabel called.

"I believe we've finished our discussion," Ramon said.

"Tell Perez he owes it to Rosa."

Ramon looked over his shoulder. "Rosa?"

"He'll know. Just tell him."

Ramon shrugged and swung the door closed behind him.

Ronnie jumped down from the table and moved swiftly toward the kitchen. "I'll fix supper. You notice how tactful I'm being? As a reward I'll expect to be filled in on all the juicy details later, Jed." She disappeared through the arched doorway and a moment later they heard the opening of the cabinets.

"Ronnie, tactful?" Ysabel smiled. "Astounding."

"She has her moments," Jed said. "Well, do I get to hear the rest of it?"

"Yes, of course. I promised you I wouldn't hold back anything once we reached San Miguel." Now that the encounter with Ramon was over, tension was leaving her and her legs felt suddenly weak. She slid down the wall and linked her hands around her knees. "It was too important to chance—" She stopped as she saw his face. "I didn't know you, Jed. Steven has been in that place for seven years. I didn't have the right—"

"Okay, okay. I can see your reasoning. It doesn't make me feel any better, but I can see it. Let's go back seven years. How did my dear father come into this?"

"We'll have to go back further than that. Twenty-four years."

"Before you were born?"

She nodded jerkily. "Marino had just taken

power, but there was already a resistance movement against his regime headed by Perez. My mother was Rosa Camina, one of the rebels Marino's troops captured and threw into the prison at Saltillo. Marino saw her one day when he was visiting the prison. She was very beautiful. You can guess the rest. I was born a year later."

"In the prison?"

"Yes, my first six years were spent in the prison. It amused Marino to visit my mother on occasion. He enjoyed her struggles and the fact that she hated him to touch her."

"He knew you were his daughter?"

"Oh yes, no one was allowed to touch my mother but him." She laughed huskily. "You think he should have shown me some affection? I told you he was a monster. I was only important as proof of his virility. However, when Steven was born six years later, it was a different matter. Marino had the usual wish for a male heir. He was planning on taking him away from my mother as soon as she had given him a good healthy start in life. Suddenly our cell was cleaner, the food better, and we were permitted time out in the sunlight. How I loved that sunlight."

She paused a moment remembering those moments of golden warmth after the darkness of the prison. "Two months later the rebels helped us escape from Saltillo, but Perez wouldn't accept Marino's children into his band. My mother refused to abandon us and fled into the jungle and hid us for over a year, dodging Marino's patrols and living off the land. Marino was enraged and sent patrol after patrol searching for us."

"How does your foster father come into this?"

"John Belfort was a protestant clergyman who had founded a mission on the southern tip of San Miguel. My mother was growing desperate and knew Marino would find us eventually if she couldn't find a place to hide us. She had heard of the mission and considered it her last hope. She persuaded John to take in Steven and me and raise us as his own."

"And your mother?"

"It was too dangerous for us to have her nearby. Children's looks change over the years, but she would have been recognized instantly. She joined the rebel forces in the hills but came to visit us as often as she could."

"Were you happy at the mission?"

She nodded. "It doesn't take much to make a child happy, and John treated us very well and even found a way to put through formal adoption papers. Yes, Steven and I were both happy." She smiled gently, remembering. "He was more like my child than my brother. After my mother left, he was all mine." She straightened her shoulders. "But you're not interested in that, are you? You asked about your father."

"He seems a compatible figure in that hellish landscape."

"Marino found out who we were—an informer at the village the mission served." She spoke quickly, eager to get it over with. "He staked out the mission and when my mother came to visit us, his troops killed her and my foster father and burned the mission."

"Good God."

"He took me and Steven back to the capital. Your father was a guest at his palazzo. At the time he was thinking of investing in several of Marino's pet industries."

"And he saw you and found his Winter Bride," he said grimly.

She nodded. "He helped me escape and told me Steven would meet us at the helicopter. It was a lie. He considered rescuing Steven too dangerous and without benefit to him. I tried to get out of the helicopter, but he held me down until we were airborne and then he began to talk. He convinced me I'd be no good to Steven in San Miguel and if I were free, I could help him."

"So he offered you a deal you couldn't refuse."

"Yes, he'd provide the money and influence to get Steven out of San Miguel if I'd do as he asked." She closed her eyes. "It seemed so simple. I didn't understand . . ."

"How could you understand? You weren't much more than a child."

"No, I was never a child. I couldn't afford that indulgence." Her eyes opened and she shrugged wearily. "I couldn't leave Steven in prison when I was free."

"Free?"

"Well, it was a prison of my own making."

"And my father's design. I notice he never managed to get Steven out of San Miguel."

"The carrot. As you said, he was very good at that. He did set up contact with Ridelez, who smuggled letters in and out of the *castillo*. I lived for those letters." She smiled bitterly. "He put Betty in charge of rationing them out to me. If I was meek and obedient, I received my reward. Once when I was particularly defiant, she burned one of his letters in front of my eyes. I never made that mistake again."

"Didn't you realize what my father was doing to you?"

"Not at first. He handled it all so cleverly. Every few months I'd have a glowing report on all the plans they were making to free Steven. About four years after I arrived at Winter Island he could see I was becoming restless and discouraged, and actually initiated an escape plan. It failed. I didn't realize it at the time, but now I believe he meant it to fail. As long as Steven was in the *castillo* I would do anything to free him. After the escape attempt I became more cynical, but he always managed to instill a tiny bit of hope in me. Hope can be a trap too." She met his gaze. "Will you forgive me?"

"Don't be absurd," he said gruffly. "I don't have anything to forgive."

"Yes, you do. I wasn't completely honest with you."

"It's a wonder you trusted me as far as you did. Your past experiences couldn't have fostered any great faith in mankind."

She said unsteadily, "I want you to know I meant what I said. I have no intention of endangering you any further than I have already. Your part in this is over. If you'll wait here until I come back, I'll—"

"No way," Jed said flatly. "I'm going with you."

She shook her head. "This is my battle. Marino already has a grudge against you and I won't put you in that kind of danger."

"You're not putting me anywhere. My choice."

He grinned. "I refuse to be used and then thrown away."

The flippant words sounded vaguely familiar and she suddenly remembered where she had heard them. "That's what Ronnie said at the hotel."

"Ronnie says a lot. Some of it even makes sense." He frowned thoughtfully. "I think we'll have to find a way to keep her off our heels. I wouldn't put it past her to insist on filming the entire rescue from inside the *castillo.*"

"And how do you intend to do that?"

He snapped his fingers. "Perez. I'll ask Ramon to take her to the rebel base in the hills after he drops us off at the shack. Then Perez's pilot can bring her along for the helicopter pickup. Filming the rebels in action should be more of a draw for her than spinning her wheels reconnoitering the *castillo.*" He straightened away from the wall. "And speaking of Ronnie, I believe I'll go and help her. I'd prefer not to start this particular endeavor with a bellyache."

She watched helplessly as he crossed the room toward the kitchen. "But I don't *need* you, Jed. My mother was a resistance fighter from the time she was fourteen. Do you think she'd let me grow up without learning how to survive and protect myself?"

He turned to face her. "A little help from your friend can't hurt."

"Friend?" she whispered.

A sudden smile lit his features with rare beauty. "Friend. We can address the more incendiary aspects of our relationship later, but I think you could use a friend now."

"Yes." She couldn't tear her gaze away from his face. "I've never had a friend except Steven."

His smile faded. "Lord, what are you trying to do to me?" He stood there looking at her for an instant before abruptly turning on his heel and entering the kitchen.

Ysabel vaguely heard Ronnie say something, but she couldn't comprehend the meaning of the words. Everything was a wild jumble of sound and sensation as she stood there looking after Jed. Everything but the one crystal clear nugget of knowledge that had struck her like a lightning bolt.

Dear heavens, how could she have been so blind? She should have realized what was happening to her. There had certainly been enough signs.

She should have guessed she loved Jed Corbin.

Ronnie lifted her gaze from the document she'd been reading on the countertop in front of her. "You're really giving Jed your home?"

"*His* home. It was never mine. I've never really had a home. Will you witness my signature please?"

Ronnie hesitated and then accepted the pen Ysabel was holding out to her, and scrawled her name on the line Ysabel had indicated. "I've never had a home either," she said wistfully. "I've never even had a country. I've always wanted—" She broke off and squared her shoulders. "Do you want me to sign anything else?"

"No, I just wanted to be sure it was done legally."
Ronnie's last words had piqued her curiosity. "I
thought you told me you were American."

"I am but there are problems. . . ." Ronnie
turned and moved toward the archway of the
kitchen.

It was clear Ronnie would not welcome any other
questions on that subject. "Where are you going?"

"Back to the cruiser to get our sleeping bags. If
we're going to spend the night here, I prefer not to
bruise my rump on that floor."

"Should I go with you? Will you need help?"

Ronnie shook her head. "Why? I'm strong
enough to carry three down-filled sleeping bags,
for goodness sake. See you." She was gone before
Ysabel could reply.

Yes, Ronnie was strong, Ysabel thought, but the
hint of vulnerability Ysabel had previously noticed
was becoming more and more clear the longer she
knew her.

She carefully took the contract and placed it in
Ronnie's knapsack, feeling as if a weight had been
lifted from her. Now she could spend these last
days with Jed with no shadow of Winter Island
hovering over her.

"You'd better give that place a good debugging."
Ronnie peered out the window of the car at the
small thatch-roofed shack across the clearing.
"You don't want any tarantulas in your sleeping
bags."

"What a comforting thought." Jed set the two

sleeping bags on the ground before helping Ysabel out of the car.

"You're sure you don't need me?" Ronnie asked. "I don't really *have* to go to Perez's base."

"And then we'd have you mooning around and playing the martyr. I believe we can survive without you until tomorrow."

"If you're lucky." Ronnie smiled impudently. "Come on, Ramon, let's get going. I have work to do."

"Presently." Ramon turned to Jed and Ysabel. "I'll be back here at seven-fifteen tomorrow morning to pick you up and take you to the *castillo*."

Surprised, Ysabel said, "You don't have to do that. It's only five miles and I have a map."

"I'll decide what I have to do," Ramon said testily. "I have no intention of helping you with the escape, but I'll drop you off a mile from the *castillo*. You've caused me enough trouble and I don't want my efforts wasted if you're stupid enough to get yourself captured." He put the car in gear and a moment later the ancient Ford was bouncing over the rutted road.

Jed picked up the two sleeping bags. "I'll store our gear and then we'll hike over to the *castillo* and check it out." He glanced at the shack. "Stay here. This place looks as if it hasn't been used in years, and Ronnie may be right about the tarantulas."

"They're usually no problem. I've dealt with tarantulas before."

"I'm sure you have." He added soberly, "I imagine you've dealt with a hell of a lot of creepy crawlies in your short life. But do me a favor and let me handle these particular pests."

Happiness flooded through her as she watched him walk toward the shack. She couldn't remember when she had ever had this precious sense of being treasured, guarded. She couldn't allow it to continue, but surely it would do no harm to let it go on for a little while.

"What, no arguments?" He glanced quickly over his shoulder and a smile lit his mobile features.

Passion, intelligence, and curiosity.

A bold, hard-edged Lancelot.

Sweet Mary, she loved him.

"No arguments."

"No guards on the ramparts," Ysabel whispered, her gaze on the twin towers of the *castillo* a few hundred yards away. "And we've seen only one guard at the gate just as Ridelez wrote me."

Jed nodded as he let the branches of the bush screening them swing back in place. "It's not a sure thing, but it all seems to check out."

She turned away from the *castillo* and started back down the path through the jungle. "Then it's a go for tomorrow."

"Yes." His brow furrowed, but he didn't speak until they were halfway back to the shack. "I've been thinking. There's no need for both of us to go after your brother."

"That's what I've been telling you," she said quickly.

"So I'll go by myself."

"You? No way," she said flatly.

"I'm more experienced and I—"

"I said no, Jed. He's *my* brother and *my* problem."

His lips tightened. "We'll see."

Good God, he was strong willed.

As strong willed as Arnold had been.

The thought came out of nowhere, sending a bolt of panic through her. She had been able to survive Arnold's domination because he had been unable to touch her emotions, but her love for Jed gave him tremendous power over her.

"Don't look like that," Jed said roughly, his gaze on her face. "It's going to be okay. We'll get him out."

They would get Steven out of his prison, but she might be edging closer to another one for herself. But why was she worrying? she thought impatiently. Jed did not love her and had made no mention of any feelings but desire and friendship. He had no place in his life for a permanent relationship. A bewildering mixture of pain and relief washed over her.

No, she wouldn't think of the future without Jed. She would enjoy these precious moments while she had them and try to make them complete in every way.

Nine

Jed came out of the hut and threw a pile of debris on the ground beside the door. His sweat-darkened pearl-gray shirt clung to his torso, his charcoal-gray cord pants were smudged with the same dust that darkened his silver hair to pewter. He was a study in gray and reminded Ysabel of a gleaming blade fashioned of the toughest steel. She felt a melting tenderness as she looked at him.

He straightened as he caught sight of her. "Where have you been?"

Her lashes lowered to veil her eyes as she strolled toward him. "No tarantulas?"

"Nary a one. I was almost disappointed. I was ready to do battle." His gaze focused on the shining braid nestled against her breast. "Why is your hair damp?"

"You refused to let me help so while you were braving nonexistent tarantulas, I was doing some reconnoitering. There's a pond about a half mile from here."

"So you went for a swim?" He frowned. "You shouldn't have gone alone. Why didn't you wait for me?"

"It was perfectly safe. The pond's surrounded by shrubbery and I grew up in the jungle, remember?" She turned and started down the path. "Let's go."

"Where?"

"To the pond. You look as hot as I felt before my swim." She looked over her shoulder at him. "Coming?"

She tried to keep her expression bland, but he must have detected something in it for his own expression changed, became arrested.

"You bet I am," he muttered as he strode after her.

Ten minutes later they arrived at the small pool. She pushed through the overhanging shrubbery and dropped down on the mossy bank. She noticed her hands were shaking and quickly folded them on her lap. "Be prepared for a shock. The water's cold after this hot sun."

"You're not going in again?"

"I'll wait here."

He caught the slight huskiness in her voice, and his eyes narrowed on her face. "Wait for what?"

She looked down at her clasped hands. "I'll just wait."

"What's this all about, Ysabel?"

She hadn't expected to feel this nervous and shy. It took an effort to answer casually, "It's all about heat. You're hot and you're going to take a swim."

She could feel his gaze on her face, then heard the rustle of clothing as he began to undress.

A moment later she heard the splash of water and raised her eyes to see Jed in the pond. The sunlight played on the shifting muscles of his tight buttocks, highlighted the corded tendons of his upper thighs.

Heat rippled through her and she found her nails biting into her palms.

He was chest-deep in water before he turned to face her. "You're right, it's cold as—" His muscles tensed. "Ysabel?"

She finished unbuttoning her shirt and slipped it off, then pulled off her boots and socks.

"May I ask what you're doing?" he asked thickly, staring at her naked breasts.

"Undressing." She wriggled out of her trousers, threw them aside, and began to unbraid her hair. "I want to get some sun." She ran her fingers through her loosened hair before lying down on the mossy bank.

"That's not all you're going to get."

His gaze on her body was generating more heat than the blazing sun. She could feel the blood running hot beneath her skin, scorching her cheeks and ripening the tips of her breasts. "I suspected as much." She had to pause to steady her voice. "Feel free to ignore me, if you wish. I don't want to force—"

"Ignore you?" He was moving toward the bank. "Are you crazy? You don't ignore a full-course meal after almost starving to death." He stepped on the bank and stood over her. His wet skin gleamed bronze in the sunlight and his arousal was stark, shocking. Drops of water fell from his body onto her sun-warmed flesh. They did not cool her. "Why now?"

She might have known he wouldn't accept without questioning. She had to quickly do something to distract him. "What difference does it make?"

"I need to know—" He broke off as she reached out and touched his calf. The muscles hardened, bunched beneath her palm.

Her hand moved along his calf, kneading, caressing.

A shudder went through him and he closed his eyes. The next moment his lids flicked open. "It does make a difference." He fell to his knees beside her. "But I don't give a damn. Not now."

He parted her thighs and moved between them. He slid with excruciating slowness into the depths of her womanhood. He was cool, heavy, hard in her warmth, and the sensation was unbearably erotic.

"Lord, it's good." His voice was shaking. "Tight. It's like nothing I've—" He reached under her, gathering her buttocks in his palms. "Hold on." He brought her high and forward as he began to plunge and drive.

A storm of emotion, sensation spiraling, whirling, giving, taking. She felt held, possessed, totally, dangerously dominated, but the *pleasure* . . .

Her hands reached out, blindly grasping his shoulders; her head thrashed back and forth on the moss. The tempo increased, the tension growing.

"Jed . . ."

"I know," he said hoarsely. "It's ripping me apart.

I need to . . ." His words trailed off as he began bucking, rotating, taking more.

"Yes." She wanted to scream, but the word came out in a whimper. "Yes, that's what—" She arched with a low cry.

Release.

A climax as violent, demanding, and wild as the striving that had gone on before.

Jed stiffened above her, the tendons visible in his throat as he clenched his teeth and threw back his head. "Ysabel!"

Her name sounded guttural, rasping, without the musical intonation she had become accustomed to hearing from him, but it filled her with primitive satisfaction. He collapsed on top of her, and her arms closed fiercely around him. *Hers.*

He did not move for a few moments, his weight endearingly heavy on her body. Then he stirred and she reluctantly loosened her clasp and let him go. His chest was still heaving as he lifted his head and looked warily down at her. "Now, what the hell was that all about?"

Not hers. He could never be entirely hers. She quickly smothered the ripple of pain the thought brought. How stupid. She had known this joy would be fleeting when she had begun. "It's very simple. I wanted this to happen."

"And you made damn sure it would." He swung off her and sat back on his heels. "Seduction."

"I'm glad it was recognizable." She made a face. "I wasn't sure I did it right."

"Oh, you did it right. You made me so hot, I was turning that cold pond into a two-hundred-degree geyser." He stiffened. "Was it that damn bargain again? Some kind of pay off?"

"No, why do you have to take everything apart?"

"It's the journalist in me. I don't buy this sudden irresistible desire for my body. There has to be a reason."

He wasn't going to let it go, and if she told him the entire truth, it would spoil these hours. She couldn't let that happen. "I suppose I'm a little afraid about tomorrow." That was certainly true. "Marino's haunted me all of my life, taken everything from me at every turn. I wanted to forget there was a possibility he might do it again."

His expression softened. "Why the hell didn't you tell me?" His hand reached out and cupped her cheek with gossamer tenderness. "You don't have to be afraid. I'll always take care of you."

Always. The bonding word rang bittersweet between them. "I didn't ask you to take care of me." She turned her head and pressed her lips on his palm. "I can do that myself."

"That's right. My role was to provide distraction." His eyes were suddenly twinkling. "I hope I proved satisfactory?"

She smiled lovingly. "Oh yes, quite satisfactory."

"I can do better."

"You can?" Her eyes widened as she glanced at his lower body. Arousal. "Now?"

"I've been known to rise to the occasion." His hand cupped her breast. "Let me show you."

Ysabel snuggled down into the sleeping bag. "I'm settled. You can turn out the lantern now."

"Not yet." He drew her closer into his arms. His embrace held none of the possessive sexuality that had been there earlier, only strength and protectiveness. "I want to talk. Something's been on my mind." He added ruefully, "Lord knows, it's a wonder I'm able to think at all. This hasn't exactly been a cerebral day."

"What's wrong?"

"I want to know what he's like."

"Who?"

"Your brother."

"Clever, loving, full of mischief." She looked gravely up at him. "Even if we had no ties, he would still be worth saving, Jed."

"Ramon's right." His hand gently stroked back her hair. "You can't be sure he's the same boy you knew seven years ago. He was only ten years old, and those years with Marino—"

"He hasn't changed," she interrupted. "If you could read his letters, you'd realize he wouldn't let Marino influence him."

"Then why did Marino visit him every month?"

"I told you Steven was clever. He realized he would gain more freedom if he and Marino had at least a tolerable relationship."

"Are you saying that kid manipulated a heavy hitter like Marino for his own ends?"

"Steven is . . . well, you'll see when you meet him."

"Just don't get your—I don't want you to be disappointed, dammit."

The words were spoken gruffly, but she was now able to see beneath the roughness to the underlying concern and felt a rush of love so exquisitely intense, it came near to pain. She instinctively drew closer to him. "Don't worry, it's going to be all right." She changed the subject. "I want you to know I've taken care of everything. I've kept my promise."

"What promise?"

"'The Winter Bride.' That's what I was doing in the kitchen with Ronnie after dinner last night. I signed over Winter Island and the painting to you and had Ronnie witness my signature."

"To hell with the Bride," he said roughly. "I'm getting sick of the lady."

"You don't mean that. She's the reason you came here."

"Is it? I'm not sure of anything anymore."

"Well, I thought I should finalize the arrangements."

"You sound like a soldier making his last will and testament before going into battle. Nothing is going to happen to you."

She wished she could be as certain as he sounded. Her euphoria was fading as the memory of the past returned. "I had to keep my promise. I told you I'd give you Winter Island."

"And I told you I didn't want the damn island. Our deal was for the painting."

"I think the island must mean more to you than you admit. It was your home. Didn't you love it as a child?"

He was silent for a long time. "I suppose I loved it. When I was a boy, I saw it through my mother's eyes and she loved every stone of the castle." He paused. "Later, I saw it only through his eyes."

"And he poisoned it for you. Neither of us have been lucky in our fathers, have we?" Her arms tightened protectively around him. "How sad that anyone has the power to take away your home."

"You sound like you're about to dissolve into tears. For Lord's sake, you never even had a home."

"But don't you see? It's much worse to lose something you've had than never to have had it at all." She laughed tremulously. "Oh dear, does that sound muddled?"

"Yes," he said huskily. "And sweet and caring."

She raised her head to look at him. She couldn't see his expression, only his light eyes glittering in the dimness. "I don't believe you've ever said anything like that to me before."

"No?" His lips gently brushed her temple. "It's the kind of thing one says . . . to a friend."

Friend. The sweetness and warmth she had felt the previous night at his words were now mixed with wistfulness. "Is it?"

"Yes." He pressed her head back into the curve of his shoulder. "Go to sleep. We're both going to need it."

Yes, she must sleep, but not for long. She must be sure to wake before Jed in the morning. She closed her eyes and cuddled closer into his embrace. Their time together was almost over and she didn't want to let him go. "I'll sleep soon . . . but this is nice, isn't it?"

She felt his lips again on her temple and his voice was a soft thunder in the darkness. "Yes, love, this is very nice, indeed."

"Where the hell do you think you're going?"

She whirled away from the door to see Jed

sitting up in his sleeping bag. She should have known no matter how careful she had been, she wouldn't be lucky enough not to have woken him. "I didn't mean to disturb you." She crossed back to his sleeping bag and fell to her knees beside him.

"What are you doing creeping around? What time is it?"

"We still have plenty of time before Señor Damirez gets here. I couldn't sleep and decided to wait outside for him."

Some of the suspicion left his tone. "Why don't you give in and let me go to the *castillo* alone? I can handle it."

"I know you can. I just—" She suddenly slid her arms around his neck.

He stiffened. "What's this all about?"

"I'm just being affectionate."

"It's a hell of a time for it." In spite of his words, his arms closed around her. "Ramon will—"

"Shhh. I want to tell you something and it helps if I'm close to you."

"What?"

"I love you."

He went still. "Ysabel, what—"

"You don't have to say anything. I just wanted to tell you, to be honest with you," she whispered, her fingers moving caressingly, searchingly, skillfully along his neck. "That's what—"

He slumped sideways, unconscious, and she caught him, lowering him back to a reclining position in the sleeping bag.

"—friends are for," she finished. She kissed him gently on the forehead, then rose to her feet and glided silently toward the door.

• • •

Five minutes later she flagged down Ramon's battered Ford on the road approaching the shack.

Ramon threw open the door to the passenger seat and peered out at her. "Where's Jed?"

"I'm going to have the helicopter stop and pick Jed up after we get Steven. He decided to stay here."

"Jed?" His tone was skeptical.

"Okay, *I* decided," she amended as she jumped into the car. "Let's go."

"I don't think—"

"Don't think," she said fiercely. "I can get Steven out of the *castillo* without Jed's help. I'm not going to let him run any more risk."

"And what if I decide you need him?"

"The decision isn't yours to make. I set up the plan and you wouldn't be here if you and Perez didn't think freeing Steven was a worthwhile goal." She leaned back in the seat. "May we leave now?"

He scowled. "I don't like— *Madre de Dios*, we don't have time to argue." He put the car in gear. "I have a message for you from Perez."

"You don't have to tell me," she said wearily. "I know we're not welcome on San Miguel. He made it clear a long time ago that we were tainted as far as the rebels were concerned."

"It's difficult to even look at a cobra's offspring without flinching away from them. Taking them to your bosom is impossible."

"Help Steven get away and we won't trouble you again."

He gave her a speculative glance. "I'd be curious to know how you kept Jed from coming along."

She didn't reply.

"He'll come after us, you know. I've watched him operate before and he's one tenacious man."

He had voiced her greatest fear. Her teeth sank into her lower lip. "I pray you're wrong."

He shrugged as he turned the car and started back the way he had come. "Prayers seem to have little value when dealing with our General Marino."

"Cripes, will you wake up!"

Jed opened his eyes to see Ronnie's concerned face above him. The concern immediately changed to relief as he regained consciousness. "You scared me. What the devil did Ysabel do to you?"

Jed flinched as he gingerly touched his neck. "Where is she?"

Ronnie helped him to a sitting position. "I assume she's at the *castillo*. Ramon got uneasy when you didn't show up and radioed the helicopter to drop down here before going on to the glade. Did she knock you on the head?"

He shook his head. "A very skilled pressure on the carotid artery and I went out like a light."

Ronnie gave a low whistle. "Talented lady."

"I can't say I wasn't warned. She told me she'd learned how to take care of herself. I'll believe her from now on." He struggled to his knees. "Let's get out of here."

"She obviously knew what she was doing," Ronnie said. "She probably could have hurt you much more if she'd tried."

"Is that supposed to console me? Hurry up and get moving."

"She only did it to protect you." Ronnie helped him to his feet. "She'd hardly sign over everything she owns to you one minute and then try to waste you the next."

"Do you think I don't know that?" His voice was harsh as he moved toward the door. "She went through living hell to protect her brother and now it seems I've been included under her cloak of protection."

She hurried after him. "We're going to the *castillo*?"

"Too late. We'll have have to keep the original plan and have the helicopter take us to the rendez-vous site in the glade. At least we'll be on hand if—" He stopped.

"If something goes wrong," Ronnie finished.

He had been too afraid to put the thought into words but knew it must be faced. "Yes, if something goes wrong."

Everything was going wrong, Ysabel thought in despair.

The guard had appeared around the corner of the building and in a moment would catch sight of the open gate and give the alarm. Dammit, he shouldn't have come back for another ten minutes!

"Run," she whispered to Steven as they darted

through the open gate toward the jungle. "Don't stop, no matter what."

"Don't worry. It would take a cannon shot to keep me here now." Steven grabbed her hand and pulled her along with him as his long legs covered the distance. "I've been training for this for seven years."

A shout behind them!

She tugged at his hand. "They've seen us. Let me go. You can run faster without me."

"Nope." His hand tightened. "I don't like it here. If they catch you, then I'd have to come back and get you. We go together."

"Steven . . ." She decided to save her breath. She had forgotten how stubborn he could be . . . and how dear. She put on speed, bearing left toward the glade.

A crashing in the shrubbery behind them!

Oh, let the helicopter be there, she prayed.

A bullet whistled by her ear!

They were closer!

"The glade's just ahead," she gasped. She risked a glance over her shoulder, but they had rounded a curve in the path and could no longer see their pursuers to judge how close they were. "The helicopter should be beyond those palms. We're going to make it!"

"Of course," Steven murmured jauntily. "Never doubted it for a moment." Nevertheless his stride took on even greater speed.

"Sure, you looked into your crystal ball and—no!"

The last word was a wail of despair as a helicopter heaved into view just in front of them, ascending, cresting the trees.

"They're leaving us!"

A crashing in the brush in front of her and Jed burst into view. "No time! This way." He dashed to the left, away from the path.

She instinctively obeyed him, dragging Steven with her.

The helicopter roared overhead, the wind from the rotors tearing at her hair.

A rat-a-tat of shots.

Were they firing at them or the helicopter?

Jed grabbed her arm, pulled her down a steep incline and then pushed her to the ground. Steven followed, falling flat on his stomach beside them.

"Why did they leave us?" she whispered.

"I told Ronnie to have the pilot take off." Jed's gaze searched the glossy shrubbery screening the path above them. "The guards were too close behind you and you'd never have gotten to the helicopter in time. Your only chance was if the guards thought you'd made it and directed their attention to the helicopter."

"But will they?" Steven asked. "What if they were close enough to see you?"

"Then we're cooked geese," Jed said. "We'll have to wait and see."

"You shouldn't have come," Ysabel said.

"You made it pretty clear I wasn't welcome," Jed said dryly. "Now shut up and we'll see if my little ruse worked."

The helicopter was turning, wheeling away toward the south.

She held her breath, waiting.

More shots, curses and then a command rang out.

Her head sank into her arms as she went dizzy with relief.

They were going back to the *castillo* to radio for air support to intercept the helicopter!

She heard a crashing of shrubbery, fading voices, and then silence. It seemed too good to be true. She was afraid to speak even after several minutes had passed.

"Stay here." Jed began to wriggle up the incline toward the path. "I'm going to have a look around."

She started after him. "I should be the one to—"

"Stay," he bit out. "If you won't take care of yourself, watch out for your brother."

She stopped and lay there, every muscle tense, her gaze searching the foliage into which he had vanished.

"A clever man," Steven said softly. "When there's more time, you must remember to introduce us."

She found her tension broken as she shot him an amused glance. "Forgive me. Amenities proved a little inconvenient."

A few minutes later Jed returned, sliding down the incline. "They swallowed it. They're heading back toward the *castillo* and didn't leave any guards."

Her breath expelled in a rush of sound. "Thank God."

Steven nudged her. "An introduction."

"My brother has been chiding me about my manners," Ysabel said. "Jed Corbin, Steven."

"Delighted to meet you." Steven solemnly nodded his head. "Particularly on this occasion."

"How do you do?" Jed said with equal gravity.

"Very well, thank you." Steven's face lit with a sunny smile. "The best I've done in seven years. What do we do now?"

"We stay here. I told the helicopter to come back in twenty minutes."

Ysabel's eyes widened. "Here?"

He nodded. "By that time the guards will be back at the *castillo* and it's the last thing they'll be expecting. The pilot will drop down, pick us up, and get out before the guards have time to make it to the glade again."

Steven laughed. "I told you he was clever, Ysabel."

"I'm glad someone appreciates me. Your sister is singularly lacking in confidence."

Ysabel said quickly. "It wasn't that I didn't think—"

"I know," he interrupted. "You wanted to do it yourself." He began crawling up the incline again. "Move closer to the glade so we won't have to waste any time when the helicopter touches down. I'll keep watch on the path to the *castillo* until it gets here."

"He's angry with you," Steven observed as he watched Jed move into the shrubbery. "Does he have cause?"

"Oh yes, he has cause."

Steven looked at her inquiringly.

"I knocked him out."

"Some sort of mating ritual?" he asked politely.

She blinked. "Why do you ask that?"

"I'm not blind, Ysabel. I spent seven years doing

nothing but studying and observing what was going on around me."

"You see too much." She studied him, liking what she saw. When she had first caught sight of Steven in the courtyard of the *castillo*, she had almost failed to recognize him. She had left a child in San Miguel and had come back to find him grown almost to manhood, only his wide-set dark eyes and tousled curly hair were familiar. Yet now she saw he still retained the gangliness of adolescence and a hint of lovable boyish mischief in his expression. Thank the Lord, Marino hadn't been able to take that away from him. She hadn't realized until then that, in spite of her denials to Jed, she'd feared that Marino, who appeared to be able to destroy everything, would also have managed to destroy Steven. "I'm beginning to wonder if my life wouldn't be more comfortable if I'd left you in that *castillo*."

He beamed. "More comfortable but less interesting."

"Well, it's certainly started out that way." She began to crawl up the incline. "Come on, Jed's right. We have to be close when the helicopter lands."

Ramon Damirez was waiting when the helicopter touched down on the dock of the village an hour later. He threw open the door and half pulled, half lifted Ysabel from the aircraft. "Get under way," he snapped at Jed. "The airways have been crackling, and the word is that Marino's mad as hell and scouring the island."

"I'm very grateful for your help, Señor Damirez," Ysabel said.

"I didn't do this for you or for your brother," Ramon said sourly. "I wanted to catch Marino with his pants down and cause him to lose face and if you don't get out of here, it will all be for nothing."

Jed jumped out of the helicopter. "We're on our way. Thanks, Ramon."

Ramon shrugged. "It's always interesting to see you, Jed." He turned and walked toward the car parked on the dock.

Jed turned to Ronnie in the backseat of the helicopter. "Turn off that camera and let's get out of here."

"Right away," she answered abstractedly as she stepped down, followed by Steven. "You go ahead and let me film Steven and Ysabel boarding the cruiser."

Jed waved at the helicopter pilot to take off. "Ronnie, dammit, do what I tell—" He grabbed Ysabel's arm and propelled her toward the cruiser. "Come on, it's quicker to do as she says than argue with her. Where's Steven? He should—" He glanced over his shoulder, and his mouth fell open. "What the—"

Steven was bowing and smiling, throwing out his chest, preening like a peacock before Ronnie's camera.

Ronnie lowered the camera, scowling. "This isn't a home movie. Will you stop . . ." She trailed off as she saw his mischievous expression and started to chuckle. "I'm going to get you for this."

"I'm giving you only my utmost cooperation."

Steven's grin was a dazzling flash in his thin face. "Should I turn so you can get my left profile. It's really my best."

"Get on board the cruiser," Jed said as he jumped down on the deck. "For Lord's sake, stop clowning."

"Steven, please," Ysabel called.

"Coming." He turned and loped swiftly toward the cruiser, tossing over his shoulder at Ronnie, "Be sure to catch my matchless grace for posterity."

"You look like a kid going on a picnic instead of escaping from prison," Ronnie said in disgust.

"I *am* going to a picnic. The entire world is a picnic after the *castillo*." He jumped on board, grabbed Ysabel and swung her around in a circle. "Isn't that so, Ysabel?"

"We're not out of it yet. You should—" She stopped as she saw his luminous expression. You couldn't dash his hopes after all he had gone through. "Yes, the world can be a picnic, Steven," she said gently. "We'll make sure it is for you."

Ronnie slung her minicamera over her shoulder and strode toward the cruiser. "Okay, since he's spoiled this footage I suppose we can leave now."

"Thank you. I'm grateful for your consideration." Jed pressed the button to up anchor and started the engine. "I was afraid you'd insist on waiting until Marino arrived on the scene to add drama."

"It's a thought, but we might risk losing the film I've already got. It's better we leave now." Ronnie boarded the cruiser. "I want to get some final shots of San Miguel receding in the distance. You'll have to handle the cruiser controls." She unslung the camera and positioned it on her shoulder again. "Even though I'm better at it than you are."

Ten

"Are we in international waters yet?" Ysabel asked.

Jed kept his gaze straight ahead on the horizon. "Yes, for about the last fifteen minutes."

"Does that mean we're safe?"

"If Marino doesn't decide to go after us and worries about jurisdiction later. It depends on how badly he wants Steven back."

She shivered. "He doesn't like anything taken away from him. He searched for us for over nine years after we escaped from Saltillo."

"Then we'd better not waste any time getting back to San Juan. We'll put in at Georgetown, Guyana, and fly to Puerto Rico from there." He glanced with exasperation at Ronnie and Steven at the front of the boat. "Look at them. You'd think they were two kids lolling on a pleasure cruise."

"I envy them."

Jed's inquiring eyes shifted to her face.

"They're both so young and so . . . tough," she said.

"Tough?"

"They have the strength to enjoy every moment of the good times and yet not let themselves be hurt by the bad. I never learned that."

"How could you?" he said roughly. "You were smothered."

"I thought patience and endurance were the only way I could win, but lately I've been wondering if I should have fought more, not let myself be robbed . . ." She paused and glanced sidewise at him. "You know I didn't want to hurt you. I didn't see any other way. . . . It was necessary."

"And was getting me in the sack necessary too?"

"No, that was for me. I wanted something for myself. I guess I wanted to say good-bye."

His grip tightened on the wheel. "I can't discuss it now. I have to get us to Georgetown."

He was still angry with her and how could she blame him? "Yes." She smiled with an effort. "Of course, that's most important. I just wanted you to know." She turned and walked quickly toward Ronnie and Steven.

"Ysabel."

She glanced back at him over her shoulder.

His eyes shimmered icicle-blue in the sunlight. "I'm sick and tired of you deciding what's 'necessary,'" he said with soft violence. "And I'm tired of you using me and I'm particularly tired of you protecting me. When we get to San Juan be prepared for a few changes."

• • •

When they arrived at San Juan the following evening, they checked in at the same hotel where Ysabel had first met Ronnie.

Jed turned away from the reception desk and crossed the lobby to where Ysabel, Ronnie, and Steven were waiting beside the elevators. He handed a key to each of them. "You three are on the fifth floor, I'm on the sixth." He turned to Ysabel and said formally, "I suggest you get some sleep. You look as if you're ready to fall in a heap."

Ronnie laughed. "Good God, I've never heard you so polite, Jed."

"I didn't want to offend the lady. I've been accused of throwing around commands."

Ysabel flinched, her hand tightening on the key. "I'm not really tired. I slept on the plane." She turned and moved swiftly toward the elevators. "I'll be fine after I have a shower."

Steven fell into step with her. "Then you won't mind going sight-seeing with me?"

She glanced out the glass doors. "Sight-seeing? It's already dark."

"Well, not really sight-seeing. I want to see *people.* I want to walk on the streets and be shoved and jostled. I want to hear noise."

"You're crazy," Ronnie said. "Noise?"

"Do you know how quiet the *castillo* was?"

Ysabel experienced a melting sympathy. He had lost so much during those years of imprisonment. "Give me twenty minutes and—"

"Jed's right, you've been through an emotional roller coaster ride in the past couple of days. You

don't need any more on your plate." Ronnie
grinned at Steven. "Go get showered and changed.
I'll find you noise and we'll even pick you up some
new duds. Of course, you won't mind me taking a
few shots of Marino's son getting his first taste of
freedom?"

"Why should I? As long as you concentrate on my
left profile." He turned to Ysabel. "You don't
mind?"

"Is it safe?" Ysabel asked Jed.

"It should be. We haven't seen any sign of pur-
suit from Marino, and Puerto Rico is American
soil. I doubt if he'd want an international inci-
dent."

"Go ahead, Steven." Ysabel followed the others
into the elevator and punched the buttons for five
and six. "But remember there are always ants at
every picnic."

"Ronnie knows how to avoid most hazards," Jed
said. "Be back by midnight."

"No arguments?" Ronnie suddenly shot him a
narrowed look. "I think you're up to something.
Now I wonder what you're going to do?"

"Nothing world shaking. I have a few phone calls
to make."

She stiffened. "Marino?"

"I thought I'd call the embassy to see if I can find
out if any citizens from San Miguel have recently
entered Puerto Rico." He lifted a brow. "I hope that
meets with your approval."

"Just so you don't go chasing after any interesting stories without me."

"I'd hardly launch an offensive until I had Ysabel
and Steven safe, would I?"

"I guess not." She frowned. "But I still—"

Her sentence was interrupted by the elevator sliding open on the fifth floor.

"Midnight," Jed said as they left the elevator. "If you're going to be later, call me."

Ysabel glanced back over her shoulder and experienced a pang of sympathy as she saw how tired he looked. It had been Jed who had arranged flights, fought with bureaucracy, and managed the details of whisking them from Georgetown to San Juan. She doubted if he had slept more than an hour since they had left San Miguel.

The door slid closed, blocking Jed from Ysabel's sight. She hurried down the hall after Ronnie and Steven.

An hour later Ysabel stepped out of the shower and slipped on the terry cloth robe supplied by the hotel. She was tying the belt as she opened the bathroom door.

"Don't be afraid."

She stopped in shock as her gaze flew across the room to where Jed sat in the easy chair by the window.

"I wanted to talk to you while we still have time."

She stood looking at him for a moment, trying to regain her composure. "Why should I be afraid?"

"Perhaps I should have said 'startled.'" He smiled crookedly. "The Amazon who single-handedly forged into the *castillo* to rescue her brother would never be afraid."

"Do Amazons have brothers? I had the idea all male children were strangled at birth or something. I'm sure I—" She broke off and drew a deep breath. She sounded like a nervous idiot with this mindless chatter. "How did you get in?"

"Sorry to invade your privacy, but I didn't want any interruptions in our discussion. I asked the desk clerk for a second key to your room when I checked in." He took out the key and placed it on the table beside him. "I won't need it any longer."

She crossed the room, sat down on the bed, and folded her hands. "I thought you were going to make some phone calls."

"Done. I called the embassy and we don't appear to have any of Marino's lads on our tail at the moment. I told them to keep alert and that I'd call back later."

She moistened her lips. "I believe I know what you're going to say. Go ahead. You have a right to be angry with me."

His hands closed on the arms of the chair. "For Lord's sake, stop bracing yourself. Do you expect me to beat you or give you a tongue-lashing?"

She smiled tremulously. "Whichever you prefer. I deserve it."

"I don't prefer either one. I thought you understood I don't abuse women and I didn't come here to do battle with you."

"Then why did you come?"

"To ask if you lied to me when you told me you loved me."

She looked down at the floor. "That's not important. I didn't mean to embarrass you. You don't have to worry—"

"Is it true?"

"Yes," she said simply. "It doesn't make any

sense, does it? We started out all wrong and what we have couldn't possibly work out. I know there are too many things against us."

"For instance."

"You still associate me with the painting and don't see me as I really am."

He looked at her, waiting.

"Temperamentally we're at opposite ends of the spectrum."

"Go on."

"I've already told you how afraid I am of cages."

"Is that all?"

"Isn't that enough?" She smiled sadly. "One more thing—you don't love me."

"Are you finished now?"

"Yes."

He stood up and strode toward the door.

She should have expected that action after her words of rejection, but it still startled . . . and hurt her. "Where are you going?"

"Back to my room. I have an answer."

"I see."

"I doubt it." He opened the door. "You seem to be deliberately blinding yourself where I'm concerned. You've built a neat little case on pure assumption because you're afraid to commit yourself to any man. The only reason you let me make love to you on San Miguel was because you thought it was temporary and therefore safe." He turned to look at her and she inhaled sharply as she saw his expression. "And I can blow every one of those assumptions out of the water. One, I can't deny any relationship with me would be confining. I'd be as possessive as hell of you, but I'm not stupid enough not to realize I'd have to make some compromises. Two, if we did have the same temperament, we'd probably be bored with each other in a month. Three, if I do still identify you with the Bride, it's because you're gutsy and beautiful and I have as much of an obsession for you as I did for her. Is that so bad?"

"No, but I—"

"And the reason I'm leaving now is that I don't have much control left. If I don't get out of here, I'd throw you on that bed and make love to you." His glance moved over her and she felt seared, breathless. "And I'm not going to do that. No more commands. If you want me, you come and get me as you did on San Miguel."

"Jed, I don't—"

"Wait." He held up his hand to check her outburst. "And you were wrong about one other thing. You didn't bother to ask me to confirm or deny that last assumption. I *do* love you, dammit!"

The door slammed behind him.

Ysabel stared dazedly at the door. Joy. She knew the sudden rush of happiness she was experiencing was dangerous, but she couldn't suppress it. Every one of the obstacles she had laid before Jed was reasonable and logical, but reason and logic had nothing to do with the fever of emotion streaming through her.

Was he right? Had she deliberately blinded herself to what they could have together because of her fear of what a commitment would mean?

Lord, she couldn't be sure of anything. Her emotions were in turmoil and the joy she was experiencing at that last terse sentence was disrupting every effort to maintain control.

I do love you.

Her palms were damp and she wiped them nervously on her cotton skirt before knocking on the door.

No answer.

It was almost midnight, and two hours had passed since he had left her room. What if he were asleep? What if he had gone out or—

The door swung open.

Jed was dressed in a terry cloth robe, his silver hair water-dampened to steel-gray. Every muscle stiffened when he saw her.

She moistened her lips. "May I come in?"

"You're damned right." He grasped her wrist and pulled her into the room. "Do you think I'm an idiot?" He slammed the door. "Sit down. I'm talking to Washington. I'll get rid of them and be with you in a minute."

"I could leave and—"

"Sit down." He strode to the nightstand and picked up the receiver and spoke tersely. "No more arguments. I need this mess cleared up. Either we go for it together as I've outlined or I do it alone." He hung up the phone and turned to face Ysabel. "Well?"

She could almost feel the tension vibrating between them. "Why are you talking to Washington?"

He ignored the question. "Why are you here?"

"Is Marino—?"

"I'm not going to talk about Washington,

Marino, or your brother. I want to know why you're here."

She swallowed hard, then said in a rush, "You said you wouldn't command me. You said I had to come to you."

He went still. "Let's be clear. You want me?"

"Yes," she whispered. "Oh, yes."

"Thank God." He moved swiftly and picked her up in his arms.

A sudden rush of panic surged through her. She had been unable to struggle against the power that had drawn her here, but now she felt as if she were being swept away from her last mooring. "There's something I have to tell you. I still don't know— There are so many problems that—"

"I don't care about the problems," he said thickly. "This is what's important now. This is one problem I know we can find an answer for." He set her on her knees on the bed. "And you must think so, too, or you wouldn't be here."

He quickly unbuttoned her blouse, slid it off her shoulders, and stood there looking at her. "I used to lie on that bunk on the cruiser and think about this." He slowly lowered his head until his mouth hovered over the right nipple.

Searing heat moved through her as his warm breath touched her.

"I remembered how you looked in the window seat with the sunlight on you." His hand reached between her thighs and began rubbing slowly back and forth.

Her stomach clenched as she felt the heat from his palm through her thin skirt.

"I'm not going to be able to hold on for very long."

Jed pushed her back on the bed and untied his robe. "It's going to be hard and fast the first time, love."

The endearment came honey-sweet through the haze of desire surrounding her.

"I don't care." She watched him shrug out of his robe and drop it on the floor. Muscular power and bold arousal. She felt suddenly small, helpless, totally female.

He noticed her reaction and went still. "If it's not what you want, tell me now. I'm not going to be able to stop if you—"

"I *do* want you. It's just hard—"

"It certainly is." His eyes were suddenly glinting with humor. "And getting harder all the time."

The easing of his tension had a soothing effect on her own. "You know what I mean. I felt . . ." She trailed off.

"Subjugated?" All trace of humor vanished from his expression. "Lord, are we back to that?" He suddenly flipped up her skirt and parted her thighs. "Since I can't leave you now, I suppose I'm going to have to lay to rest that bogey."

"How are you—?" She arched up off the bed as she felt his thumb press on the sensitive nub of her womanhood. "Jed!"

"Like this."

He began a circular motion that made her bite her lip to keep from crying out.

"I'm not forcing you, am I?" The demand came fierce and intense.

"No . . ."

His other hand moved down and two fingers

sank deep while his thumb continued the circular motion. "This is what you want. Right?"

She barely heard the question. The sensations he was arousing were indescribably erotic and her breath was coming in little pants.

"Right?" he asked again.

"Yes."

"Progress." His voice was guttural and she was vaguely aware of his face above her, flushed, heavy with sensuality as he mounted her. "Think. Am I giving you what you want?"

Hard warmth nudging at the apex of her womanhood. She clenched, trying to close around him. "Jed, this is—" She made a sound low in her throat as he entered her and then stopped just within. "No!"

"You want me gone?"

"You know that's not what I mean."

He moved a fraction farther. "Then tell me what to do. You're not subjugated. You're the one in control. I'm not moving until you tell me. Until you command me."

Heavy fullness, but not enough. She was burning, throbbing. "Jed, for heaven's sake, *move.*"

"Not yet." He laughed desperately. "Lord, did I say that?"

She bucked, trying to take more of him, but he held himself immobile. "Command."

"All right!" Her hands clutched his shoulders. "Dammit, Jed, I'm commanding you. Move!"

He moved, exploded, cupped her buttocks, and drove deep.

She cried out and her legs closed fiercely around him.

It was the same as before yet different, passionate yet sweeter. It went on forever, but when the climax came it was still too soon.

The languor was deeper, more complete, and even when he left her, she still felt joined to him.

It was several moments before she could speak. "It's very difficult, isn't it?"

He chuckled. "I disagree. There's nothing simpler." He nuzzled her ear. "Or more pleasant."

"No, I didn't mean . . ." She raised herself on her elbow to look at him. "Sex makes things more . . . it's too strong . . . it gets in the way of judgment."

He stiffened. "We made love, not sex. I thought we had gone beyond that point."

"We have. I mean I think—" She stopped. "I guess I'm still confused."

"About what? I thought I'd made my position quite clear."

She was silent.

"Talk to me."

"I suppose I'm afraid," she whispered. "You're much stronger than Arnold and . . . oh, I know you're nothing alike but—"

"The cage," Jed finished. "Like father, like son." His fingertips gently brushed the plane of her cheek. "I've tried to be as honest as I can with you. It's going to have to be your decision whether you trust me or not, but don't expect me not to stay close and try to influence you to my way of thinking even if it takes the next fifty years." He rolled over and mounted her again, plunging smoothly into the heart of her. "In the meantime, I believe I'll reinforce my position."

• • •

The phone was ringing.

Why didn't Jed answer it? Ysabel wondered drowsily.

The ring sounded again, igniting a frisson of uneasiness within her.

She opened her eyes and immediately stiffened.

No Jed. The early morning sunlight revealed that the pillow beside her was indented, still bearing the impression of his head. But he was no longer there.

The phone rang again and she rolled over and reached for the receiver, conscious that the cool sheets held no lingering warmth.

"Hello."

"How long ago did he leave?" Ronnie demanded.

"What?" The uneasiness came into sharp focus. She slowly sat up and brushed the hair from her eyes.

"He left without me, dammit," Ronnie fumed. "Well, he's not going to get away with it. How much headstart does he have?"

"I don't know what you're talking about. What's happened?"

"You don't know?" Ronnie muttered something beneath her breath. "Jed's gone after Marino."

The blood turned to ice in Ysabel's veins. "How do you know?"

"I have Brooking from the CIA standing in front of me. Jed's been pulling strings in Washington and got them to send Brooking to pick us up."

"I don't understand."

"Jed wanted us protected from Marino and arranged with Brooking to place us in protective custody while he went off and played games with the General."

"What . . . games?"

"Cat-and-mouse, with Jed being the bait. He thought with Marino so hopping mad, it would be a perfect time to lure him into a trap."

Ysabel closed her eyes. "Dear Lord."

"Well, he can't get away with it. He *needs* me. I'm not going to hole up in some crummy hotel in West Virginia while he—"

A man's voice came suddenly on the line. "Mrs. Corbin, this is Paul Brooking. I've dispatched a man to your room to pack your bags and escort you to the lobby at your earliest convenience. Miss Dalton, your brother, and I will meet you in forty-five minutes, if that will be okay." In spite of the courteous phrasing, there was a note of crisp resolution in the man's tone.

"Where is Jed?"

"We're not at liberty to divulge his exact whereabouts. He did give me a message for you. He said if you follow him to San Miguel, it will make his position only more hazardous since your presence may keep him from obtaining help from the rebels. He'll contact you as soon as possible. Forty-five minutes, please." The connection was broken.

She replaced the receiver with a trembling hand. Why hadn't she anticipated Jed's move when it was so in character? Lancelot to the rescue. The cold seemed to be surrounding her, filling her. Not, it wasn't cold that was icing through her; it was fear. She got out of bed and stumbled toward the bathroom. Forty-five minutes . . .

Suddenly fear was replaced by anger. How dare Jed do this to her? He had been so blasted angry and indignant about her trying to protect him and yet he was doing the same thing, risking his life and—

His life. The anger disappeared as quickly as it had come. Dear Lord, Jed could die. Marino could kill him as he had killed so many others and there wasn't one thing she could do about it. She had never felt so helpless in her life. The reservations and bewilderment that had plagued her the previous night seemed minuscule in the glaring light of the knowledge that she could lose him.

Jed could die.

No, she wouldn't accept that possibility. She would just have to wait and have faith that he would come back to her. Sweet Heaven, that waiting wouldn't be easy.

In the meantime, she would have to fight down her fear and take charge of the aspects of the situation that were still open to her. She couldn't help Jed, but she would keep Steven and Ronnie safe.

Ysabel moved quickly across the lobby toward Ronnie and Steven. Standing beside them wearing a rumpled khaki suit was a tall young man with reddish-brown hair and freckles.

She stopped before him. "Mr. Brooking? I'm Ysabel Corbin. Your agreement with Jed calls for certain protective measures for us?"

Ronnie muttered, "It calls for us to be stashed in no-man's-land."

Steven sympathetically touched her arm. "I've been there before. No-man's-land isn't amusing, but we'll make the best of it."

"How long will we be under guard?" Ysabel asked Brooking.

"Hopefully not more than a few weeks. My superior has made assurances to Jed that you be kept absolutely secure, but that doesn't mean we have to keep you in a cell. I've located quite a nice small motel in West Virginia that even has a swimming pool. I assure you we'll make your stay as comfortable as possible."

Ronnie snorted.

Ysabel nodded. "I believe my friend's reaction is similar to my own. I've just freed my brother from one prison and I have no intention of placing him in another."

"I've told you that—"

"I've heard what you told me. Now I think you'd better listen to me." Her tone reflected her inflexibility. "I have no objection to accepting your help in keeping us safe. However, it will be my choice where that guardianship will take place."

Brooking frowned. "You're being very foolish. We have a breadth of experience you don't possess." He tried to temper the sharpness of his voice. "Look, trust me. Let us do our job."

"I'm not stupid, Mr. Brooking, and I'm not going to make the mistake of endangering our lives. I want very much to live."

Ronnie's gaze was narrowed on Ysabel's face. "What do you have in mind?"

"I know a place that's isolated, that will allow us

a maximum amount of freedom and can be defended with little effort."

"What place?"

Ysabel smiled. "Why, we're going back to Winter Island."

Ronnie gave a low whistle as they moved up the path toward the front door of the castle. "I'm impressed. Jed never talked about his home, but I didn't expect Windsor Castle."

"Jed has a few problems with Winter Island." Ysabel glanced at Steven. "You've been very quiet since we left the boat. Is something wrong?"

He forced a smile. "What could be wrong?"

"That's what I'm asking."

His gaze went back to the stone turrets. "I'll get used to it."

"Why would—?"

Ronnie grabbed Ysabel's arm. "Good God, who's the giantess?"

Betty Starnes had opened the door and stood in the entryway, her features contorted with gloating malice. Ysabel braced herself for the coming encounter but managed to smile. "It's funny you should say that. Jed told me she reminded him of the giant's wife in 'Jack and the Beanstalk.'"

"So you've come crawling back. I knew you would." Betty's glance fell on Ronnie and Steven, and her lips curled. "Who are these people? I won't accept them here. They'll have to leave. Mr. Arnold wouldn't permit—"

"Choose any room you like," Ysabel told Ronnie

as she stepped around Betty and entered the foyer. "Heaven knows the castle has enough of them."

Betty followed them. "I told you they couldn't stay."

Ysabel turned to Steven. "You're bothered because it reminds you of the *castillo*, aren't you?" As he started to protest, she shook her head. "Don't worry about it. It may take you awhile to become adjusted. Jed has a cabin on the south side of the island. It's not very luxurious, but you'd be comfortable. Why don't you move in there?"

Steven looked relieved. "Could I? I've had enough of castles for the time being. You wouldn't mind?"

"I thought I'd had enough of them too until I realized a place is only what you make it." She smiled. "Go on and get settled. Follow the path south and down the hill. You can't miss it. We'll expect you back for dinner at seven."

He gave her a grateful grin and bolted out of the castle.

"Who is that?" Betty demanded. "What right do you have telling him where he can stay?"

Ysabel ignored her questions. "We have four other guests, security men who are reconnoitering the island at the moment, but they should be here within the hour. Make sure they have comfortable accommodations."

"Are you giving me orders?" Betty drew up to her full height. "Have you forgotten who I am?"

"A bully and bad-tempered shrew comes immediately to mind," Ysabel said coolly. "But you're also the housekeeper here and have certain duties I expect you to perform."

Livid color spotted Betty's cheeks. "I don't take orders from you."

"Don't you? You'll either take them or have your stay made very uncomfortable."

"Good God, I feel like I'm at Manderley," Ronnie said. "Where did you get this poor man's Mrs. De Winter, Ysabel?"

"I inherited her. She goes with the castle."

"It's no wonder you signed the castle over to Jed."

"You what!" Betty's eyes were suddenly blazing at Ysabel. "You couldn't have done that. Mr. Arnold—"

"Stole Winter Island from Jed," Ysabel finished. "And now it's his again."

"You slut, you've destroyed everything." Betty grabbed Ysabel's arm, her nails biting cruelly into flesh. "Just because he takes you to bed and—"

"Release my arm." Ysabel enunciated the words clearly and coldly. "I told you once you were never to touch me again."

Betty's grasp tightened.

Ronnie took a protective step forward.

"Stay out of it, Ronnie," Ysabel said without looking at her. "I'll handle this."

"Ungrateful whore," Betty said between her teeth.

"Once more. Let me go."

"You always did—"

Ysabel's right fist rammed into the large woman's stomach.

"Whumpf!" The sound that came from Betty's lips was like the air being let out of a pricked balloon.

As the housekeeper's grasp loosened, Ysabel

jerked free, stepped to the side, and knifed a karate chop to the woman's neck. The house-keeper toppled like a felled tree.

Ysabel was vaguely shocked at the fierce satis-faction surging through her at the sight of the woman lying unconscious on the floor. She hadn't realized until this moment how much she had needed retribution for the torment of those years.

She smiled serenely as she stepped over the woman's crumpled body and moved toward the stairs. "You might like the room next to mine, Ronnie. It's decorated in yellow and is a bit more cheerful than— What are you laughing at?"

"Whipped cream." Ronnie hopped over Betty and ran up the stairs after Ysabel. "Dear Lord, and I thought you were whipped cream!"

"They're on Winter Island?" Jed gazed at Brook-ing, stunned. "Why the devil did you put them there?"

"I didn't voluntarily put them there. I had a safe house set up in West Virginia, but I had no choice. Ysabel Corbin refused to go anywhere else." Brook-ing shrugged. "Other than putting them in a cell, which we didn't think you'd appreciate, we had to go along with her. She appeared to object to her brother being in close confinement."

"Yes, she would," Jed said absently. But why Winter Island? he wondered. Ysabel certainly had no love for the place and Betty Starnes would delight in making her life hell. "It's been four weeks. Why wasn't I told of the change of plan?"

"The determined Ms. Corbin again. She said the

change would worry you and you didn't need any additional baggage if you were going into danger. She seems quite protective of you."

"Oh, she's definitely protective." He grimaced. "Sometimes painfully so. Are you through with my debriefing?"

Brooking nodded. "Get the hell out of here." He smiled. "And thanks, Corbin. We might have brought Marino down in time, but I prefer sooner to later."

"So did I. I did it for myself as much as for you." Jed turned to go. "I want my life back in order."

"Jed?" Ysabel whispered, her hand tightening on the receiver. She felt dizzy with the relief and joy coursing through her. "Are you all right?"

"Fine," he said curtly. "What the devil are you doing there with that witch?"

"Betty? She's not here any longer. She left three days after we arrived."

"Why?"

"She didn't like it here anymore." She rushed on, "You're sure you're not hurt? What about Marino?"

"Perez has him, and his political base is crumbling. Tell Ronnie I shot the capture myself and got it right side up."

"I'll tell her."

"I'm on my way. I'll be in Seattle by noon and the island by one-thirty."

"I'll be waiting."

"Will you?" His voice sounded husky. "That sounds good. No one's ever said that to me before." The next moment the connection was broken.

"He's coming." Ysabel put down the receiver and turned to Ronnie, who was sitting in an easy chair across the library. "He should be here within a few hours."

"What about Marino?"

"Perez has him. Jed said to tell you he'd done the camera work on the capture and he'd got it right side up."

"I should have been there." Ronnie shrugged. "Well, maybe Jed will feel guilty enough about cheating me out of the story that he'll owe me." Her lips tightened grimly. "And I'll make damn sure he knows it."

"I'm sure you will." Ysabel turned and moved toward the door.

"Where are you going?"

"I have preparations to make before I go meet him." She glanced thoughtfully at the picture of the Winter Bride over the fireplace. "I believe it's time we cleared up a few things."

She was standing beneath a tree, the bitter winter wind lifting her hair against the velvet hood as Jed walked up the path toward the castle.

She saw Jed stop in midstride as he caught sight of her and she braced herself. Then he was moving swiftly toward her.

"I thought you'd finished with this charade," he said, his gaze traveling over the long ivory velvet gown she wore and then to the ermine-trimmed cloak. "I suppose you have a reason for all this?"

She nodded. "I wanted to make a statement."

"And that is . . . ?"

She met his gaze. "That I'm not afraid of what the Winter Bride means to you anymore. I've had a long time to think about it and I've decided she's no competition. I have sufficient presence and strength of purpose to stand on my own."

"That's what I've been trying to tell you."

She smiled. "I had to reach my own conclusions. You may have noticed I'm a little stubborn."

His lips twitched. "It's come to my attention."

"I thought it had." Her smiled faded. "I was very angry with you for going after Marino, you know."

"It was something I had to finish. He would always have been there in the background haunting you."

"But you didn't let me help." She gestured toward the gown. "You treated me as if I were that child in the painting. You tried to protect me, for goodness sake. It wasn't fair when you get so angry with me for doing the same thing."

"That was different. I had no choice but to—" He stopped. "You're right, it was the same scenario. I was just the prime player. I couldn't stand the thought of you being hurt."

"So you sent Brooking to put us in a nice neat box while you went out to brave Marino." She held up her hand as he opened his mouth to protest. "I'll accept what you did this time and I've come to terms with the fact that your job means there may be moments of danger and worry in the years ahead."

He went still. "Years?"

She smiled. "I believe you mentioned fifty or so?"

"At least." His voice was thick. "If that's not too much commitment for you."

"It's not enough. No, don't touch me." She took a hasty step back as he moved toward her. "I have some more to say and I can't think when you touch me."

"Neither can I. Talk and it better be quick. Lord, it's been *four* weeks, love."

Dear heavens, she wanted to go into his arms. "I want to tell you why I came back to Winter Island."

"Brooking told me," he said impatiently. "And I've been thinking about it. Perhaps we should stay here until we're sure all of Marino's goons have been rounded up. I'll hire private bodyguards after Brooking's men leave. Later we'll buy a condo in Seattle."

"I've already taken care of that. Brooking put me in touch with four ex-Special Forces people and they'll arrive tomorrow morning."

"I suppose I should have expected you to beat me to the punch," he said dryly.

"We're going to pay them very well and I expect them to stay a long, long time."

"You may not need them for more than six months or so. Marino's finished on San Miguel and Perez will make sure his forces are disbanded."

"We'll need them." She smiled serenely. "I've decided, if you continue in this extremely dangerous profession, you're going to need a sanctuary to come home to. When we're traveling, we'll probably take one of the men with us."

"A bodyguard?" He looked outraged.

"Listen to me, Jed." A steely note entered her tone. "You *will* be as safe as I can make you. I won't have it any other way."

"I won't be tailed by a—" He suddenly started to laugh. "Lord save me from a protective woman."

"This protective woman will help the Lord save you from more dangerous hazards than herself."

"I'm beginning to wonder if there is anyone more hazardous."

"And there's another reason why I came back to Winter Island." She paused. "I want to be married here."

"What?" His eyes widened. "You can't be serious. You went through hell in that castle."

"That's why I want the marriage to take place there." Her words tumbled out. "Don't you see? We need new memories to replace the old. Beautiful memories. Your mother loved the island and so did you at one time. If you let Arnold destroy that for you, then you lose again." She added in a whisper, "And so will I. We're stronger than that, Jed. We don't need to run away again."

He gazed at her a moment. "You really want this?"

"I want to make this place our own. I want Winter Island to belong to you again. I told Ronnie I'd never had a home, but it's important to put down roots. You already have roots here and we only have to make them healthy and strong again." She smiled tremulously. "What do you think the Winter Bride would have done back in medieval times? She wouldn't have packed up and moved to a condo in Camelot. She would have lived in her castle and changed circumstances to suit herself."

He took a step forward and gently touched her cheek. "But, as you've often told me, you're not the Winter Bride."

"I was wrong." A brilliant smile lit her face. "I'm the *new* Winter Bride and you'll have to reckon with me as her husband did her."

He lifted her chin with his fingers as he looked into her eyes. "Oh, I will," he said tenderly. "And love you and cherish you for as long as we live."

"You will?" she whispered.

His eyes suddenly twinkled with mischief. "I wouldn't dare do anything else."

THE EDITOR'S CORNER

Next month LOVESWEPT celebrates heroes, those irresistible men who sweep us off our feet, who tantalize us with whispered endearments, and who challenge us with their teasing humor and hidden vulnerability. Whether they're sexy roughnecks or dashing sophisticates, dark and dangerous or blond and brash, these men are heartthrobs, the kind no woman can get enough of. And you can feast your eyes on six of them as they alone grace each of our truly special covers next month. HEARTTHROBS—heroes who'll leave you spellbound as only real men can.

Who better to lead our HEARTTHROBS lineup than Fayrene Preston and her hero, Max Hayden, in **A MAGNIFICENT AFFAIR**, LOVESWEPT #528? Max is the best kind of kisser: a man who takes his time and takes a woman's breath away. And when Ashley Whitfield crashes her car into his seaside inn, he senses she's one sweet temptation he could go on kissing forever. But Ashley has made a habit of drifting through her life, and it'll take all of Max's best moves to keep her in his arms for good. A magnificent love story, by one of the best in the genre.

The utterly delightful **CALL ME SIN**, LOVESWEPT #529, by award-winner Jan Hudson, will have you going wild over Ross Berringer, a Texas Ranger as long and as tall as his twin brother, Holt, who thrilled readers in **BIG AND BRIGHT**, LOVESWEPT #464. The fun in **CALL ME SIN** begins when handsome hunk Ross moves in next door to Susan Sinclair. He's the excitement the prim bookstore owner has been missing in her life—and the perfect partner to help her track down a con artist. But once Ross's downright neighborly attention turns Susan inside out with ecstasy, she starts running scared. How Ross unravels her intriguing mix of passion and fear is a sinfully delicious story you'll want to read.

Doris Parmett outdoes herself in creating a perfect HEARTTHROB in **MR. PERFECT**, LOVESWEPT #530. Chase Rayburn is the epitome of sex appeal, a confirmed bachelor who can charm a lady's socks off—and then all the rest of her clothes. So why does he feel wildly jealous over Sloan McKay's personal ad on a billboard? He's always been close to his law partner's widow and young son, but he's never before wanted to kiss Sloan until she melted with wanton pleasure. Shocking desire, daring seduction, and a friendship that deepens into love—a breathtaking combination in one terrific book.

Dangerously sexy, his gaze full of delicious promises, Hunter Kincaid will have you dreaming of **LOVE AND A BLUE-EYED COWBOY,** LOVESWEPT #531, by Sandra Chastain. Hunter knows he can win the top prize in a motorcycle scavenger hunt, but he doesn't count on being partnered with petite, smart-mouthed Fortune Dagosta. A past sorrow has hardened Hunter's heart, and the last person he wants for a companion for a week is a beautiful woman whose compassion is easily aroused and whose body is made for loving. Humorous and poignant, the sensual adventure that follows is a real winner!

Imagine a man who has muscles like boulders and a smoky drawl that conjures up images of rumpled sheets and long, deep kisses—that's Storm Dalton, Tami Hoag's hero in **TAKEN BY STORM,** LOVESWEPT #532. A man like that gets what he wants, and what he wants is Julia McCarver. But he's broken her heart more than once, and she has no intention of giving him another chance. Years of being a winning quarterback has taught Storm ways to claim victory, and the way he courts Julia is a thrilling and funny romance that'll keep you turning the pages.

Please give a rousing welcome to new author Linda Warren and her first LOVESWEPT, **BRANDED,** #532, a vibrantly emotional romance that has for a hero one of the most virile rodeo cowboys ever. Tanner Danielson has one rule in life: Never touch another man's wife. And though he wanted Julie Fielding from the first time he saw her, he never tasted her fire because she belonged to another. But now she's free and he isn't waiting a moment longer. A breathlessly exciting love story with all the wonderfully evocative writing that Linda displayed in her previous romances.

On sale this month from FANFARE are three marvelous novels. **LIGHTS ALONG THE SHORE,** by immensely talented first-time author Diane Austell, is set in nineteenth-century California, and as the dramatic events of that fascinating period unfold, beautiful, impetuous Marin Gentry must face up to the challenges in her turbulent life, including tangling with notorious Vail Severance. Highly acclaimed Patricia Potter delivers **LAWLESS,** a poignant historical romance about a schoolteacher who longs for passionate love and finds her dreams answered by a coldhearted gunfighter who's been hired to drive her off her land. In **HIGHLAND REBEL,** beloved author Stephanie Bartlett whisks you away to the rolling hills and misty valleys of the Isle of Skye, where proud highland beauty Catriona Galbraith is fighting for her land and her people, and where bold Texas rancher Ian MacLeod has sworn to win her love.

Also available this month in the hardcover edition from Doubleday (and in paperback from FANFARE in March) is **LUCKY'S LADY** by ever-popular LOVESWEPT author Tami Hoag. Those of you who were enthralled with the Cajun rogue Remy Doucet in **THE RESTLESS HEART,** LOVESWEPT #458, will find yourself saying Ooh la la when you meet his brother, Lucky, for he is one rough and rugged man of the bayou. And when he takes the elegent Serena Sheridan through a Louisiana swamp to find her grandfather, they generate what *Romantic Times* has described as "enough steam heat to fog up any reader's glasses."

Happy reading!

With warmest wishes,

Nita Taublib

Nita Taublib
Associate Publisher/LOVESWEPT
Publishing Associate/FANFARE

Don't miss these fabulous Bantam Fanfare titles
on sale in JANUARY.

LIGHTS ALONG THE SHORE
by Diane Austell

LAWLESS
by Pat Potter

HIGHLAND REBEL
by Stephanie Bartlett

Ask for them by name.

LIGHTS ALONG THE SHORE

BY DIANE AUSTELL

The Gentrys. They had left the comforts of the Old
South and come to California, a sunlit Eden where
ranchers put down roots and grew wealthy, while
beautiful young women such as Marin Gentry
danced until dawn and dreamed of undying love.
But ahead was turmoil no man or woman could
foresee: the discovery of gold, with its lure of easy
money and easier death, the dizzying growth of
bawdy San Francisco, the gathering stormclouds
of Civil War. . . .

*   *   *

Marin Severance is reunited with her brother-in-law, Vail, for the first time since the night, several years before, when she was still unmarried, and he seduced her. . . .

Stuart had gone to San Francisco four days ago to buy parts for the water pump, and she expected him home for supper.

There were sounds of horses pounding past the side of the house and Stuart's voice calling to Mateo. Then boots on the wooden floor of the back porch and the kitchen door banging open. Marin swung around with flour still on her hands and a smile of greeting on her face. Coming in the door were Stuart, Michael, and, just behind them, Vail Severance.

She picked up a towel, wiped her hands, and moved to Stuart for a kiss of welcome. She said something to Michael, although she couldn't hear her own voice for the roaring in her ears.

What could she do? Where could she look? She must speak to him, look at him, smile at him. It would seem very odd if she didn't. But all the blood in her body seemed to have rushed into her head. Oh, God, how could she explain to Stuart why the sight of his brother upset her so? She forced herself to look into Vail's eyes, and the buzzing in her head made her think she was going to faint.

There was nothing at all in those clear gray eyes but friendliness and the mildest sort of interest, the kind of interest a man might show on greeting his brother's wife, a girl he had known slightly at some time in the distant past. She put out her hand because she had to, felt the corners of her mouth go up in a smile, and heard him say, "Hello, Red."

Somewhere she found the strength to say, "Welcome, Vail. Have you come home to stay?"

Supper went off smoothly, and by the time Luz served the cobbler and cream, Marin had decided that she was going to live after all. Stuart appeared to have noticed nothing odd about her behavior, perhaps because he had been pulling off his coat when she spoke to Vail and had his back turned. Michael had simply stood there and smiled as he always did when he saw her, and as for Vail—Papa and Ethan had clearly been right about the memory-destroying properties of alcohol, for he obviously recalled nothing about that night. He treated her just as he always had, perhaps a little more courteously because of her increased age and status, but that was all. . . .

After supper Marin sat down by the parlor fire in her favorite chair, the one Rose had used in the old days, and picked up a shirt of Stuart's to mend, thinking with relief that she now had a little time to compose herself. She looked up, and the thread snapped in her fingers. Vail had come into the room alone.

Damn the man! Why couldn't he go look at the horse or the pump, or tend to some other masculine matter? Why did he have to follow her in here, where there was no one else to share the burden of conversation? The business of rethreading the needle took her close attention, but she watched him covertly, noticing the way he moved, the vitality in his face.

He sat down opposite her and stretched his booted legs toward the flames, and she busied herself with the torn frill of Stuart's shirt, wondering how long she could maintain this domestic pose and make some kind of polite conversation.

Her mind fumbled, searching for something to say, and Petra came in with her gliding, boneless walk. She set the tray bearing coffeepot and cups on the table next to Marin and, as she bent forward, murmured, "Carey is still awake, Miss Marin. Should I bring him down?"

Marin snatched at the suggestion like a drowning man at a straw. Young as he was, Carey, had a gift for drawing all eyes to him—in this case, away from her.

"Yes, bring him down," she said gratefully.

"How is my mother?" Vail asked suddenly. He was lighting a cigar and frowning into the fire.

It was a safe subject. "Not well," Marin answered, her eyes on her sewing. "Will you see her before you leave?"

"I can't."

She looked up, thinking of Ethan. It was such a sorry, stupid situation. "Surely your father wouldn't object? She's quite ill, I think."

"He would object—which would make it worse for her." A smile crossed his face, and Marin caught her breath at the bitterness in it. Without watching her hand, she shoved the needle through the cloth and jabbed her finger. A bright drop of blood appeared, and she scowled and put it to her mouth.

Vail's smile became genuine. "You looked like a child when you did that. I keep forgetting how young you are."

It was the first personal remark he'd made, and it unnerved her so much that she almost dropped the shirt. He must not have noticed though, for he went right on, "This is the first chance I've had to apologize for my conduct the night of Celia's party. I was very rude."

The finger remained in her mouth; her heart seemed to come to a standstill. He did remember, then, and he was apologizing for *rudeness*?

She was not thinking clearly, but she heard him say, "I had a bad case of hurt feelings that night, as you probably know, and I'm sorry to say I got very drunk. I seem to remember leaving you on the dance floor with Gerald Crown, which I certainly would never have done in my right mind. I hope you've forgiven me."

Her heart began to beat again. He thought he'd left her with Gerald.

"Oh, I forgave you immediately. Gerald is charming and a very good dancer." She picked up the coffeepot and began to pour with a steady hand.

He winced. "I deserved that. My brother married a quick-witted lady as well as a beautiful one. I wasn't so lucky."

He was thinking of Celia. Should she mention her? No, better not. Petra brought in Carey, and Marin took him on her lap with relief. Vail leaned forward and looked him over.

"A handsome boy," he said finally.

She warmed to the praise, as she always did to any kind words for Carey.

"Yes," she said, and laughed. "Forgive me, I can't be modest. I think he's handsome, too." She set the child on the floor, and he immediately went up on all fours and started to rock so vigorously that he tumbled over and lay there crowing. Then he struggled up and tried again to move forward.

Vail took his cup, watching with a smile.

"I suppose Father is delighted."

"Oh, yes. He was miffed at first when we didn't name the

baby after him, but he got over it when he decided that Carey looked like him. At present he's very pleased with me."

"And with Stuart, too, I imagine. Well, Stuart always had the knack of pleasing him. I never did." He said it without self-pity, but Marin remembered Celia's words: "His father hurt him badly."

She picked up her own cup. "Except for your mother, no one agrees with him. My mother thinks Carey strongly resembles her family, the Landrinis, and my father says he looks like me."

Carey raised his head as if he knew he was being discussed, and Vail watched him, moved—even more than he had expected—by emotions hard to analyze. Shame at what he had done to this girl, so innocent and so drunk—it had all been his fault. Respect for her cool courage when she first saw him in the kitchen and her poker player's skill when she showed him her baby. Surprising sadness at the knowledge that, for the baby's sake and for hers, he could never claim the boy as his own. Wonder at the simple fact of the child. There might be other children in the world who were his, but none he knew of, none so certain as this little boy looking up at him with great black eyes shining.

He said, "Your father is right. At least he has his mother's wonderful eyes."

Carey spared her the necessity of a reply. He made a tremendous effort, lifted one tiny hand, brought it forward, and moved the knee behind it. Then he moved the other hand and knee, lifted his head, and chortled.

"Oh!" Marin breathed. "He's done it, he's crawling. Oh, he's been trying so hard!"

Carey began to move faster and faster now that he had figured out the difficult business, traveling in a circle with a triumphant gurgling laugh until he fell in a heap at Vail's feet. Immediately he got up and sat down again with a plop. The man above him extended a finger for him to tug, and the child examined it interestedly, talking to himself in a cooing babble.

Vail looked down at the soft, dark curls. "So now I am an uncle. God, it makes me feel old."

"Ethan is an uncle, too, but he doesn't know it."

"No word at all?"

"Nothing. I think about the knife fights and the hangings in the gold camps. Sometimes I'm afraid . . ."

"Don't be. Ethan can take care of himself. He's a good man in a fight, but he doesn't look for trouble."

"It need never have happened. Papa will never be well, and Mama—she is not herself at all. It was all so stupid . . ."

"Tragedies usually are, because people are stupid. I'm in the camps fairly often. I have business there at times. Ever since I heard about Ethan, I've kept an eye out for him, and I'll continue to."

With a rush of gratitude she said, "Oh, it would mean so much just to know that he's alive, even if he doesn't come home." Impulsively she added, "It's a shame Logan didn't know you were coming. Next time let us know, and I'll make sure she's here."

Why had she said that? Only minutes before she had been hoping never to see this man again, and now she had invited him to come back and to meet Logan in her home, which would make an enemy of Malcolm if he found out. No help for it now. She couldn't take back the invitation, not with him smiling at her like that and the warm light again in his eyes.

"That's very kind. I worry about Logan, trapped in that house."

"There's no place else she'd want to be, not now, with her mother sick. But—do come back. Seeing you will help her, I'm sure of that."

LAWLESS

BY PATRICIA POTTER

Author of RAINBOW

"One of the romance genre's finest talents . . ."
—Romantic Times

IN LAWLESS, Patricia Potter tells the dramatic and compelling story of a brave schoolteacher and the lawless outcast who becomes her protector. When Willow Taylor refuses to sell her land to powerful rancher Alex Newton, legendary gunfighter Lobo is hired to drive her away. But his attempts go awry as he ends up rescuing members of her "family" from disasters, including a fire. Worse, he's shocked to discover that Willow is unlike the heartless women he's known only too well. As more gunslingers arrive, wreaking havoc in a once peaceful community, Willow remains undaunted, and Lobo feels the heat of unbidden longing for this strong and beautiful survivor.

In the following excerpt, Lobo has broken off with Newton and has temporarily sided with Willow. Under a velvet-dark sky, he finds himself opening up to her as he never had with anyone before. . . .

* * *

"Why do they call you Lobo?"

He shrugged. "The Apache gave me the name. It seemed as good as any."

"As good as Jess," she asked, using his real name.

He scowled. "I told you he died."

Willow didn't say anything, but the silence was heavy with her doubt.

He turned away from her. "Lobo fits, lady. Believe me."

"The wolf is a social animal," Willow said as if reading out of a book. "He mates for life."

Lobo turned and stared at her icily. "Unless he's an outcast, chased from the pack, and then he turns on his own kind." There was no self-pity in the observation, only the cold recital of fact.

"Is that what happened?"

Lobo felt his gut wrench. He'd never meant to say what he had, had not even consciously thought it before. A cold dread seeped through him as he realized how much control of himself he was losing.

"Lady, I've done things that would make you puke. So why don't you go back to your nice little house and leave me alone."

Willow hesitated. She sensed the turmoil in him, and it echoed her own churning emotions.

"I don't care about the past," she finally said.

He laughed roughly. "I don't scare you at all?"

She knew he wanted her to say yes. She knew she should say yes. She should be fearful of someone with his reputation, his life. But she wasn't.

"No," she answered.

"You don't know me, lady."

"Willow."

He shook his head. "And the last thing you should do is be out here with me."

"Were you with the Apache long?" she asked softly.

It was a sneaky question, and he stiffened. "Long enough."

She sensed his withdrawal, if it was possible that he could distance himself any farther than he already had. The kiss might never have happened, except it was so vivid in her mind.

Her hand went out to his, which was wrapped around the post. "Thank you for staying."

His hand seemed to tremble, and she wondered if she imagined it.

"You may not be grateful long," he replied shortly.

"You will stay, then?"

"A few days," he replied. "But the town won't like it. I'm usually not welcome."

"If Alex can hire you, I can," she answered defiantly.

"But Newton has money, and you . . . ?"

Again the implication was clear, and she knew she was flushing a bright red. She hoped the moonlight didn't reveal it, but she saw the glint in his eye and knew her hope was in vain.

Her thoughts turned to what had been nagging her, to the violent death that had occurred just hours earlier. "You won't have to fight Marsh Canton if you stay?" Her hand shook slightly as she posed the haunting question.

The glint was still in his eye. "A lot of folks been waiting for that."

"I've never seen anyone so . . . fast," she whispered.

His right hand went to his neck. "He's good. Aren't you going to ask me if I'm just as good?"

She didn't want to think of him that way. She preferred thinking of him hauling her poor bull Jupiter from the burning barn. "No," she whispered.

"That's what I do, you know," he persisted almost angrily. "I'm no hero like you want to believe. I'm a killer just like Canton. You want to know how many people I've killed?"

Her gaze was glued to his eyes, to the swirling, dangerous currents in them. She heard the raw self-contempt in his voice, but what he was saying didn't matter to her, not to the way she felt about him, not to the way she wanted to . . . touch and hold and . . .

"I was twelve when I first killed," he continued in the same voice. "Twelve. I found I was real good at it."

His eyes, filled with tormented memories and even rage, blazed directly at her. And she felt her need for him deepen, felt her heart pound with the compulsion to disprove his reason for self-derision.

But she couldn't move, and she had no words that wouldn't anger or hurt or sound naive and silly. That, she sensed, was what he was waiting for so he could have a reason to leave. The currents running between them were stronger than ever, and Lobo was willing her to say or do something to destroy it, but she was just as determined not to. Silence stretched between but something else too, something so strong that neither could back away.

If she'd offered compassion or sympathy, Lobo could have

broken through her hold on him. But she gave neither. Instead, he was warmed by the unfamiliar glow of understanding, of unquestioning acceptance. He basked in it, feeling whole for the first time that he could remember. All of a sudden he realized this was what he'd been searching for, not freedom but something so elusive he'd never been able to put a name to it.

And it was too late. His insides churned and twisted with pure agony as he realized that one indisputable fact. He carried too much trouble with him. His reputation, which he had so carefully nurtured, was a noose around his neck. The older he got, the more the rope tightened. He could live with that, but he couldn't live with the fact that it was also a noose around the neck of anyone foolish enough to care for him.

He forced himself to take a step back, to fight his way out of the moment's intimacy, one deeper than any he'd ever shared with a person, deeper than when he plunged his manhood into a woman. Christ!

"Lady, you should run like hell!" His voice was harsh, grating. "You and those kids don't need the kind of grief I bring."

She worried her lips as she sought for something to say, to somehow express her belief in him, but before she found the words, he spoke again.

"And I sure as hell don't need *you*." He emphasized the last word as if trying to convince himself, and once again he stepped back.

"Jess . . ."

His mouth seemed to soften for a moment, and he hesitated. But then his mouth firmed again, and his eyes turned hard. He bowed slightly, mockingly. "If I'm going to be of any use to you, ma'am, I'd better turn in."

He strolled lazily back to the barn and disappeared within, leaving Willow feeling desolate and alone.

HIGHLAND REBEL

BY STEPHANIE BARTLETT

Author of HIGHLAND JADE

Catriona Galbraith was a proud highland beauty who would do anything to stop a tyranical laird from possessing her homeland and heritage. Ian McLeod was the bold Texas rancher who swore to win Cat's love from the moment he laid eyes on the bewitching young woman. But Ian didn't know the dangerous secret that beckoned to Cat night after night: a secret that could sow the seeds of rebellion and destroy their passion.

* * *

Squares of yellow lamplight stained the snow in front of the church. Ian pulled his muffler tight against an icy gust as he followed Colin up the stone steps. The wind grew even colder after the winter sun went down.

Warm air, thick with the smells of wool and sweat, surrounded Ian as he sidled through the door. The interior droned with excited voices, all talking at once. Small wonder after the last two days.

Mindful of his height, he settled himself in the back pew. Colin patted his shoulder, then moved on up the aisle toward the front, where he could see and hear. For once Ian was glad to be an outlander. Without the old man around, the other crofters still ignored him for the most part, and that was fine with him. He didn't much want to talk to anybody anyhow. All they wanted to do was crow about their victories over the sheriff's men.

He wondered whatever had possessed the courts to send another officer the next day, trying to serve papers of some kind. Fin Lewis made short work of the man, a kid really. Tossed his papers in the muddy snow and escorted him to the edge of the estate at the point of his pike.

Ian rubbed at a smudge of soot staining his fingers. Most of the crofters wanted justice for themselves, but Fin liked to fight, bullying men who were outnumbered a hundred to one. Granddaddy always said there was one in every bunch.

He shrugged. At least they were on the same side, although he'd wager Fin was only concerned for himself. He didn't like the fella, didn't trust him at all. He only hoped he wouldn't ever have to depend on him.

Damn! The last thing he wanted to think about tonight was Lewis. Crossing his arms over his chest, he glanced around the room. The stone building was packed, every pew full to overflowing with men. Many of them even brought their families.

Gavin Nicolson smiled and waved from a few rows up. The man nudged the woman beside him. His daughter Belag. She turned and smiled back over her shoulder, but her cheeks crimsoned and she turned away when he tipped his hat. A pretty little thing with brown hair and dark eyes. She'd make some man a fine wife.

He tried to image himself with her, then shook his head to clear it. He knew he'd never love another woman, Catriona owned his heart, and she always would. Maybe someday his memories would dim enough so he could marry and have a family. But he didn't hold out much hope.

If only he could see Cat again, just for one night. He ached to put his arms around her, hold her, make love to her. His lips twisted into a bitter smile. She didn't love him, didn't want him, or she would have agreed to marry him. No, he might as well wish for a magic pony to ride him home to Texas across the clouds.

He wondered how things were at the Braes, with the poor crops and the hard winter. He missed Fergus and Jennet, Effie would be growing, and Geordie must be almost a man. It would be spring again soon. Two years since Granddaddy died. Two years since he met Catriona in the graveyard. Would his life ever be right again?

The voices around him subsided, bringing him out of his reverie. Dugald Purcell mounted the steps and took his place in the pulpit. "My friends, we have faced the enemy, and we have won!" A cheer echoed back from the rafters. Purcell went on, but Ian listened with only half an ear.

He shifted on the hard seat, trying to think how to go about settling these folks down. He could understand them being happy about running the sheriff out of town, but he figured they didn't know how dangerous it was to fight the law. And a lot of good it did him to warn Purcell, telling him what Campbell had said about the army; he just nodded and said, "Aye." And now he'd called another meeting.

A second figure moved up the pulpit steps, a woman, her head shrouded with a tartan shawl. Ian leaned forward. He'd seen her somewhere before. The image flashed through his mind, the woman who spoke with Purcell just before the fight at the bridge.

He caught the last of Purcell's words, something about a visitor who wanted to help plan their next actions. The slender figure stood beside the crofter. Facing the crowd, she lifted the shawl from her head, letting it drop to her shoulders. Black curls cascaded over her shoulders, and even from the back of the church, Ian could see her eyes were a deep blue. But it wasn't until she smiled that he knew for sure.

Catriona.

Catriona lay back on the musty coverlet and closed her eyes. Weariness weighed on her, the tension of the last few days and nights aching in every muscle. She was grateful for a bed and a room where she could be alone. On the edge of sleep, Ian's face floated before her.

Her body throbbed a bittersweet tune. She'd hungered for the sight of him for months, months with no word even to say he was still alive, still on Skye. Then tonight, as they ushered her into a church full of nervous crofters, there he stood.

She gave the speech Hugh helped her write before she left the Braes, rallying them to the cause and answering their questions. But she never forgot for a moment that he was there, sitting in the back, head and shoulders taller than the men around him. She tried not to look, but she couldn't keep her eyes away from him. The way his fine blond hair strayed across his forehead, shining in the lamplight, the way his handsome face eased into a smile and his eyes never strayed from her face as she talked. When the meeting ended and the crofters poured out the tall doors, she looked for him, but he'd vanished.

Cat rolled over and punched a hollow in the hard pillow. If only they could talk. Now, with them both fighting the lairds, he had to understand why she couldn't marry him and go to America, why she had to stay on Skye.

She tossed onto her back and stared up at the rafters. Tomorrow she'd find him, go to the forge and talk to him, tell him how much she missed him, how much she loved him. A smile curved her lips and she closed her eyes. Everything would be the way it was last spring.

A soft tapping startled her from a near-dream. It was late. Most of the guests at the lodge were asleep. She slid off the narrow bed and crept to the door, keeping her feet silent and her voice low. "Who is it?"

"Ian. Let me in."

Her pulse raced and she could scarcely catch her breath as she undid the bolt and pulled him into the room. In one move her arms went around his neck and her lips pressed his. Ian's love surrounded her, his hands traveling over her body. A delicious warmth swirled in her head and down her spine to end pulsing low in her belly.

Then Ian's hands cupped her shoulders and pushed her down onto the bed. She lay back and held up her arms to receive him.

He stood beside the bed, frowning down at her. "Cat, how can you do this?"

She sat up, her face flushed with disappointment and confusion. "Do what?"

"Risk your life traveling the countryside, stirring up trouble. Fighting the constables. I saw you in the crowd the other day. And the march to Dunvegan tomorrow. What will happen if you get caught?"

Anger kindled from the ashes of her longing. "Why, the same that'll happen if they catch you, I suppose."

His mouth opened, then snapped shut. "You don't

understand. The sergeant we chased out of here yesterday said the sheriff has asked for the army to come in."

The army. Purcell hadn't mentioned it. She bit her lip, trying to keep from shivering. "I hope they do," her voice sounded stronger than she felt.

He stared at her, his eyes wide. "A real war. Is that what you want?"

She tossed her head. "The eyes of the country are on Skye. The public is with us now. If they send the army against us, it can only make our case stronger."

He tossed up his hands and paced across the threadbare carpet. "And if they shoot people, will it be worth it then? Do you want to die?"

Cat swallowed before she answered. "Do you?" Her voice sounded hollow in her ears. She knew she didn't want to die, nor did she want him to die. Would the army really shoot to kill?

He stopped pacing and turned to face her, holding his clenched fists at his sides. "It's not the same thing. I'm a man."

"I've not forgotten what you are, but I see no difference in the risks we take." She pushed herself to her feet. "And you, what reason have you to fight the lairds? You're not even a proper Scotsman."

His full lips thinned to a hard line. "I'm a Macleod, same as the landlord. It's my duty to help make things right."

She took a step closer and planted her hands on her hips. "Aye, and I'm a Galbraith and a Macdonald. And I was born and bred a crofter, not a rich landowner from America."

The heat of his body reached out to her, but she fought the urge to touch him. Weariness settled over her again, and she looked away. It was no use—he'd never understand. "I've no more to say to you, so I'll thank you to leave now." She turned her back to him.

"Cat." His voice caressed her, and the longing pulsed deep in her belly. His hands slid down her shoulders and turned her toward him. Without a word he drew her into his arms and kissed her deep and long. Cat melted against him.

His mouth still clinging to hers, he lifted her and carried her to the bed.

She lay back, savoring the sweetness of his mouth on hers, the weight of his body pressing against her. His fingers fumbled at the buttons of her blouse, and then his hand cupped her breast, the work-roughened palm brushing her nipple. She gasped with pleasure as his lips followed his hand.

She traced the planes of his muscles, trailing her fingers down his chest. Trembling, she unfastened his trousers, slid her hands inside, and caressed the feverish hardness of his body.

He moaned and kissed her, pressing his lips against her mouth, her eyelids, her throat. His hands slid beneath her skirt, bunching the hem up around her waist. When his fingers smoothed the length of her thighs, caressing her secret pleasure, she arched against him in a fever of desire.

Unable to wait any longer, she tugged his trousers down over his buttocks and guided him inside her, closing her eyes and moaning as he filled her. She rose to meet him, wave after wave of pleasure washing through her, until she cried out, spilling over with delicious agony. Somewhere above her she heard him moan, and felt him collapse on top of her.

Without opening her eyes she slid her arms around him, holding his body against her. *Ian.* His name danced through her mind, making its own melody of love. Nothing else mattered.